James Napier

Folk lore

Or, Superstitious beliefs in the west of Scotland within this century

James Napier

Folk lore

Or, Superstitious beliefs in the west of Scotland within this century

ISBN/EAN: 9783741193903

Manufactured in Europe, USA, Canada, Australia, Japa

Cover: Foto ©Andreas Hilbeck / pixelio.de

Manufactured and distributed by brebook publishing software
(www.brebook.com)

James Napier

Folk lore

FOLK LORE:

OR,

SUPERSTITIOUS BELIEFS IN THE WEST OF SCOTLAND WITHIN THIS CENTURY.

WITH

AN APPENDIX,

SHEWING THE PROBABLE RELATION OF THE MODERN FESTIVALS OF CHRISTMAS,
MAY DAY, ST. JOHN'S DAY, AND HALLOWEEN, TO ANCIENT SUN
AND FIRE WORSHIP.

BY

JAMES NAPIER, F.R.S.E., F.C.S., &c.,

*Author of " Manufacturing Art in Ancient Times," " Notes and Reminiscences
of Partick," &c., &c.*

PAISLEY: ALEX. GARDNER.

1879.

CONTENTS.

APPENDIX.

PREFACE.

THE doctrine taught concerning Satan, his motives and influence in the beginning of this century, supplied the popular mind with reasons to account for almost all the evils, public and private, which befell society; and as the observed ills of life, real or imaginary, greatly outnumbered the observed good occurrences, the thought of Satan was more constantly before the people's mind than was the thought of God. Practically, it might be said, and said with a very near approach to truth, that Satan, in popular estimation, was the greater of the two; but theoretically, the superiority of God was allowed, for Satan it was believed, was permitted by God to do what he did. It was commonly said, "Never speak evil of the Deil, for he has a long memory." This Satanic belief gave rise to a great amount of Folk Lore, and affected the whole social system. Historians who take no account of such beliefs, but regard them as trivialities, cannot but fail to represent faithfully the condition and action of the people. Folk Lore has thus an important historical bearing. Every age has had its own living Folk Lore, and, beside this, a residuum of waning lore, regarded as superstitious, and so it is at the present day. When we speak of the Folk Lore of our grandfathers and great-grandfathers, we believe that we are speaking of beliefs which have past away, beliefs from which we ourselves are free; but if we consider the matter carefully we will find that in many respects our beliefs and practices, although somewhat modernized, are essentially little different from those of last century. Among the better educated classes it may be said that much of the superstitions of former times have passed away, and as education is extended they will more and more become eradicated; but at present, in our rural districts especially, the old beliefs still linger in considerable force. Many think that the superstitions of last century died with the century, but this is not so; and as these notions are curious and in many respects important historical factors, I have thought it worth while to jot down what of this Folk Lore has come under my observation during these last sixty years.

In this collection I do not profess to include all that may come under the head of Folk Lore, such, for example, as the reading of dreams and cups, spaeing fortunes by cards or other methods—that class of superstitions by which designing persons prey upon weak-minded people.

One principal object which I had in view in forming this collection, was that it might supply a nueclus for the further development of the subject. The instances which I have adduced belong to one locality, the West of Scotland, and chiefly the neighbourhood west of Glasgow, but different localities have different methods of formulating the same superstition. By comparison, by separation of the local accretion from the constant element, an approach to the original source and meaning of a superstition may be obtained.

I have hope that the Folk Lore Society, just instituted, will consider such details and variations, and endeavour to trace their history and origin, and fearlessly give prominence to the still existing superstitions, and exhibit their degrading influence on society.

FOLK LORE.

CHAPTER I.

INTRODUCTORY.

THE primary object of the following short treatise is to give an account of some of those superstitions, now either dead or in their decadence, but which, within the memory of persons now living, had a vigorous existence, at least in the West of Scotland. A secondary object shall be to trace out, where I think I can discover ground for so doing, the origin of any particular superstition, and in passing I may notice the duration in time and geographical distribution of some superstitions. But, on the threshold of our inquiry, it may be of advantage to pause and endeavour to reach a mutual understanding of the precise meaning of the word Superstition—a word apparently, from the varied dictionary renderings given of it, difficult to define. However we may disagree in our definitions of the word, we all agree in regarding a superstitious tone of mind as weak and foolish, and as no one desires to be regarded

as weak-minded or foolish, we naturally repel from ourselves as best we can the odious imputation of being
superstitious.   There are few who seek to know what
superstition in its essence really is ; most people are
satisfied to frame an answer to suit their own case, and
so it happens that we have a multiplicity of definitions
for the word, many of which are devoid of scientific
solidity, and others have not even the merit of intelli-
gibility.   A recent definition, extremely elastic, was pro-
pounded by a popular preacher in a lecture delivered
before the Glasgow Young Men's Christian Association
and reported in the newspapers,—" Superstition is Scepticism," which may be legitimately paraphrased "Superstition is not believing what I believe."   Although this
definition may be very gratifying to the self-pride of
most of us, we must nevertheless reject it, and look for
a more definite and instructive signification, and for this
end we may very properly consult the meanings given in
several standard dictionaries and lexicons, for in them we
expect to find precision of statement, although in this instance I believe we shall be disappointed.   Theophrastus,
who lived several centuries before the Christian era,
defines "Superstition" according to the translation given
of his definition in the *Encyclopædia Metropolitana*, as
" A cowardly state of mind with respect to the supernatural," and supplies the following illustration: " The
superstitious man is one, who, having taken care to
wash his hands and sprinkle himself in the temple,
walks about during the day with a little laurel in his
mouth, and if he meets a weasel on the road, dares not
proceed on his way till some person has passed, or till
he has thrown three stones across the road."

Under "Superstition," in the *Encyclopædia Metropolitana*, the following definitions are given :—

1st.—Excess of scruple or ceremony in matters of religion : idle worship : vain reverence : a superfluous, needless, or ill-governed devotion.

2nd.—Any religious observance contrary to, or not sanctioned by, Scripture or reason.

3rd.—All belief in supernatural agency, or in the influence of casual occurrences, or of natural phenomena on the destinies of man which has no foundation in Scripture, reason, or experience.

4th.—All attempts to influence the destiny of man by methods which have no Scriptural or rational connection with their object.

Walker's Dictionary :—

" Unnecessary fear or scruple in religion : religion without morality : false religion : reverence of beings not properly objects of reverence : over-nicety : exactness : too scrupulous."

Chambers' Dictionary :—

" A being excessive (in religion) over a thing as if in wonder or fear : excessive reverence or fear : excessive exactness in religious opinions and practice : false worship or religion : the belief in supernatural agency : belief in what is absurd without evidences : excessive religious belief."

These dictionary meanings do not, of course, attempt to decide what should be the one only scientifically correct significance of the term, but only supply the varying senses in which the word is used in literature and in common speech, but they suffice to show that it is used by different persons with different significations, each person apparently gauging first his own position, and defining superstition as something which cannot be brought to tell against himself.

After pondering over the various renderings, it occurred to me that the following definition would embrace the whole in a few words : *Religion founded on erroneous ideas of God.* But when I set this definition alongside the case of an otherwise intelligent man carrying in his trousers' pocket a raw potato as a protection against rheumatism, and alongside the case of another man carrying in his vest pocket a piece of brimstone to prevent him taking cramp in the stomach ; and when I consider the case of ladies wearing earrings as a preventive against, or cure for, sore eyes ; and, again, when I remembered a practice, very frequent a few years ago, of people wearing what were known as galvanic rings in the belief that these would prevent their suffering from rheumatism, I could not perceive any direct connection between such superstitious practices and religion, and the construction of a new definition was rendered necessary. The following, I think, covers the whole ground : *Beliefs and practices founded upon erroneous ideas of God and nature.* With this meaning the term "Superstition" is employed in the following pages, and if the definition commend itself to the reader, it will at once become apparent that the only way by which freedom from superstition can be attained is to search Nature and Revelation for correct views of God and His methods of working. Notwithstanding our pre-

tensions to a correct religious knowledge, a pure theology, and freedom from everything like superstition, it is
strange yet true, that, if we except the formulated reply
to the question in the Westminster Catechism, "What is
God," scarcely two persons—perhaps no two persons—
have exactly the same idea of God. We each worship a
God of our own. In one of the late Douglas Jerrold's
"Hedgehog Letters" he introduces two youths passing
St. Giles' Church at a lonely hour, when the one ad-
dresses the other thus :—"The old book and the parson
tell us that at the beginning God made man in his own
image. We have now reversed this, and make God in
our image." A sad truth, although not new; Saint Paul
made a similar remark to the philosophic Athenians ;
but the remark applies not to this age or to Saint
Paul's age alone—its applicability extends to every
age and every people. As Goethe remarks, "Man
never knows how anthropomorphic he is." Our
minds instinctively seek an explanation of the cause
or causes of the different phenomena constantly
occurring around us, but instinct does not supply
the solution. Only by patient watching and consideration can this be arrived at; but in former ages scientific
methods of investigation were either not known, or not
cared for, and so men were satisfied with merely guessing
at the causes of natural phenomena, and these guesses
were made from the standpoint of their own human
passionate intelligence. Alongside the intelligence everywhere observable in the operations of nature they placed
their own passionate humanity, they projected themselves
into the universe and anthropomorphised nature. Thus
came men to regard natural phenomena as manifestations

of supernatural agency; as expressions of the wrath or pleasure of good or evil genii, and although in our day we have made great advances in our knowledge of natural phenomena, the majority of men still regard the ways of providence from a false standpoint, a standpoint erected in the interests of ecclesiasticism. Churchmanship acts as a distorting medium, twisting and displacing things out of their natural relations, and although this influence was stronger in the past than it is now, still there remains a considerable residuum of the old influence among us yet. For example, we are not yet rid of the belief that God has set apart times, places, and duties as specially sacred, that what is not only sinless but a moral obligation at certain times and places becomes sinful at other times and places. Ecclesiastical influence thus familiarises us with the distinctions of secular and sacred, and we hear frequent mention made of our duties to God and our duties to man, of our religious duties and our worldly duties, and we frequently hear religion spoken of as something readily distinguishable from business. But not only are these things separated by name from one another, they are often regarded as opposites, having no fellowship together. Hence has arisen in many minds a slavish fear of performing at certain times and in certain places the ordinary duties of life, lest by so doing they anger God. In certain conditions of society such belief, erroneous though it be, may have served a useful purpose in restraining, and thereby so far elevating a rude people, just as now we may see many among ourselves restrained from evil, and influenced to the practice of good, by beliefs which, to the enlightened among us, are palpable absurdities.

Before reviewing the superstitious beliefs and practices of our immediate forefathers, we may, I think, profitably occupy a short time in gaining some general idea of the prominent features of ancient Pagan religions, for without doubt much of the mythology and superstitious practice of our forefathers had a Pagan origin. I shall not attempt any exhaustive treatise on this subject, for the task is beyond me, but a slight notice of ancient theology may not here be irrelevant. The late George Smith, the eminent Assyriologist, says :—

"Upwards of 2000 years B.C. the Babylonians had three great gods—*Anu*, *Bel*, and *Hea*. These three leading deities formed members of twelve gods, also called great. These were—

1. Anu, King of Angels and Spirits. Lord of the city Eresh.
2. Bel, Lord of the world, Father of the Gods, Creator. Lord of the city of Nipur.
3. Hea, Maker of fate, Lord of the deep, God of wisdom and knowledge. Lord of the city of Eridu.
4. Sin, Lord of crowns, Maker of brightness. Lord of the city Urr.
5. Merodash, Just Prince of the Gods, Lord of birth. Lord of the city Babylon.
6. Vul, the strong God, Lord of canals and atmosphere. Lord of the city Mura.
7. Shama, Judge of heaven and earth, Director of all. Lord of the cities of Larsa and Sippara.
8. Ninip, Warrior of the warriors of the Gods, Destroyer of wicked. Lord of the city Nipur.
9. Nergal, Giant King of war. Lord of the city Cutha.
10. Nusku, Holder of the Golden Sceptre, the lofty God.

11. Belat, Wife of Bel, Mother of the great Gods. Lady
     of the city Nipur.
12. Ishtar, Eldest of Heaven and Earth, Raising the
     face of warriors.

Below these deities there were a large body of gods,
forming the bulk of the Pantheon; and below these
were arranged the Igege or angels of heaven; and the
anunaki or angels of earth; below these again came
curious classes of spirits or genii, some were evil and
some good."

The gods of the Greeks were numbered by thousands,
and this at a time when—according to classical scholars
—the arts and sciences were at their highest point of
development in that nation. Their religion was of the
grossest nature. Whatever conception they may have
had of a first cause—a most high Creator of heaven and
earth—it is evident they did not believe he took anything to do directly with man or the phenomena of
nature; but that these were under the immediate control of deputy-deities or of a conclave of divinities, who
possessed both divine and human attributes—having
human appetites, passions, and affections. Some of
these were local deities, others provincial, others national, and others again phenomenal: every human
emotion, passion and affection, every social circumstance,
public or private, was under the control or guardianship
of one or more of these divinities, who claimed from
men suitable honour and worship, the omission of which
honour and worship was considered to be not only
offensive to the divinities, but as likely to be followed by
punishment. The vengeance of the deities was thought
to be avertable by the performance of certain propitiatory

deeds, or by offering certain sacrifices. The kind of sacrifice required had relation to the particular department over which the divinity was supposed to be guardian; and these deeds and sacrifices were in many cases most gross and offensive to morality. The phenomena of nature, being under the direction of one or more divinities, every aspect of nature was regarded as an expression of anger or pleasure on the part of the divinities. Thunder, lightning, eclipses, comets, drought, floods, storms—anything strange or terrible, the cause of which was not understood, was ascribed to the wrath of some divinity; and men hastened to propitiate, as best they might, the divinities who were supposed to be scourging or threatening them. These deputy-gods were supposed to occupy the space between the earth and moon, and, being almost numberless and invisible, their worshippers held them in the same dread as if they possessed the attribute of omniscience.

For the purpose of guiding men in their relations towards these gods, there existed a large body of men whose office it was to understand the divinities, their natures and attributes, and direct men in their religious duties. This body of men acted as mediums between the gods and the people, and not only were they held in high esteem as priests, but frequently they attained great power in the State. Often this priestly incorporation had greater influence and control than the civil power; nor is this to be wondered at, when we remember that they were supposed to be in direct communication with the holy gods, in whose hands were the destinies of men.

The sun, the giver and vivifier of all life, was the primary god of antiquity, being worshipped by Assyrians,

Chaldeans, Phœnicians, and Hebrews under the name
of Baal or Bell, and by other nations under other names.
The priests of Baal always held a high position in the
State. As the sun was his image or symbol in heaven,
so fire was his symbol on earth, and hence all offerings
made to Baal were burned or made to pass through the
fire, or were presented before the sun. Wherever, in
the worship of any nation, we find the fire element, we
may at once suspect that there we have a survival of
ancient sun-worship.

The moon was regarded as a female deity, consort of
the sun or Baal, and was worshipped by the Jews under
the name of Ashtoreth, or Astarte. Her worship was of
the most sensual description. The worship of sun and
moon formed one system, the priests of the one being also
priests of the other.

Apart from the priestly incorporation of which we
have spoken, there was another class of men who assumed knowledge of supernatural phenomena. These
were known as astrologers or star-gazers, wizards, magicians, witches, sooth-sayers. By the practice of certain
arts and repetition of certain formula, these pretended
to divine and foretell events both of a public and private
nature. They were believed in by the mass of people,
and were consulted on all sorts of matters. By both the
civil and ecclesiastical authorities their practices and
pretensions were sometimes condemned, and themselves
forbidden to exercise their peculiar gifts, but nevertheless the people continued to believe in them and consult them. Their pretensions were considerable, extend-
ing even to raising and consulting the spirits of the
dead.

This leads me to notice the ancient belief concerning the souls of the departed. By almost all nations, Jews and Gentiles, there was a prevailing belief that at death the souls of good men were taken possession of by good spirits and carried to Paradise, but the souls of wicked men were left to wander in the space between the earth and moon, or consigned to Hades, or Unseen World. These wandering spirits were in the habit of haunting the living, especially their relations, so that the living were surrounded on every side by the spirits of their wicked ancestors, who were always at hand tempting them to evil. However, there were means by which these ghosts might be exorcised. A formula for expelling wicked spirits is given by Ovid in Book V. of the Fasti :—

"In the dread silence of midnight, upon the eighth day of May, the votary rises from his couch barefooted, and snapping his fingers as a sure preventative against meeting any ghost during his subsequent operations, thrice washing his hands in spring water, he places nine black beans in his mouth, and walks out. These he throws behind him one by one, carefully guarding against the least glance backwards, and at each cast he says, 'With these beans I ransom myself and mine.' The spirits of his ancestors follow him and gather the beans as they fall. Then, performing another ablution as he enters his house, he clashes cymbals of brass, or rather some household utensil of that metal, entreating the spirits to quit his roof. He then repeats nine times these words, 'Avaunt ye ancestral manes.' After this he looks behind, and is free for one year."

Some nations in addition to a personal formula for laying the ghosts of departed relatives, had a national ritual for ghost-laying, a public feast in honour of departed spirits. Such a feast is still held in China, and also in Burmah. In 1875 the following placard was posted throughout the district of Rangoon, proclaiming a feast of forty-nine days by order of the Emperor of China :—

" There will this year be scarcity of rice and plenty of sickness. Evil spirits will descend to examine and inquire into the sickness. If people do not believe this, many will die in September and October. Should any people call on you at midnight, do not answer; it is not a human being that calls, but an evil spirit. Do not be wicked, but be good."

But I do not propose to write a treatise on Pagan theology, nor do I propose to trace in historical detail the progress through which Christian and Pagan beliefs have in process of time become assimilated, when I have occasion, I may notice these things. I intend, as I said at the beginning, to deal with superstition, no matter from what source it may have arisen, recognising superstition to be as already defined—beliefs and practices founded upon erroneous ideas of God and the laws of nature. In many things, I believe, we are yet too superstitious, and our popular theology, instead of aiding to destroy these erroneous beliefs, aids them in maintaining their vitality. Orthodox Christians believe in a general and also in a special providence ; the ancients, on the other hand, believed that all events were under the control and direction of separate and special divinities, so that when praying for certain results, they addressed the divinity having control over that phenomenon or circumstance by which they were affected, and when their desires were gratified, they expressed their thankfulness by offerings to that divinity. If their desires were not granted, they regarded that circumstance as a token of displeasure on the part of that divinity, and besought the aid of their priests and soothsayers to discover the reason of his anger, and offered sacrifices and peace offerings. Now, orthodox Christians in the same circumstances pray to God for special and personal blessings, and when they are granted, they feel grateful, and sometimes express their gratitude. A common method of expressing this gratitude is by giving something to the church. Thus we find in our church records entries like the following :—

		£	S.	D.
From ——— ———, As a thank-offering for the recovery of a dear child.				———
,, ——— ———, Peace-offering for reconciliation with an old friend,				———
,, ——— ———. Offering for the preservation of a friend going abroad.				———
,, ——— ———, Thank-offering for a fortunate transaction in business.				———

Such offerings are remarked upon favourably by the leaders of the Church, and regarded as examples worthy of being imitated by all pious Christians. But should the prayers not be granted, there is no gift. The non-fulfilment of their desires is regarded perhaps not altogether as an evidence of God's displeasure, but at least as a token that what was asked it was not His pleasure to grant. They make little enquiry concerning the real cause of failure, but take credit to themselves for humbly submitting to God's will. This unenquiring submission is often, however, both sinful and superstitious. Every result has its cause, and it is surely our duty, as far as observation and reason can guide us, to discover the causes which operate against us. The great majority of the afflictions and misfortunes which befall us are punish-ments for the breakage of some law, the committal of some sin physical or moral, and this being the case, it behoves us to find out what law has been transgressed, what the nature of the sin committed. This principle is acknowledged by our religious teachers, but the laws which have been broken, have not been wisely sought after. The field of search has been almost exclusively the moral, or the theological field; whereas the correct rule is, for physical effects, look for physical causes; for moral effects, moral causes. This rule has not been followed. A few cases illustrative of what I mean will clearly de-monstrate the superstitious nature of what is a widely diffused opinion among the religious societies of this country at the present time.

Forty-six years ago, when cholera first broke out in this country, it was immediately proclaimed to be a judgment for a national sin; and so it was, but for a sin against physical laws. I well remember the indignation which arose and found expression in almost every pulpit in the country, when the Prime Minister of that day, in reply to a petition from the Church asking him to pro-claim a national fast for the removal of the plague, told his petitioners to first remove every source of nuisance by cleansing drains and ditches, and removing stagnant pools, and otherwise observe the general laws of health, then having done all that lay in our power, we could ask God to bless our efforts, and He would hear us. All sorts of absurd causes were seriously advanced to account for the presence of this alarming malady. One party discovered the cause in a movement for the disestablishment of religion. Another considered it was a judgment from God for asking the Reform Bill. The Radicals proclaimed it to be a trick of the Tories to prevent agitation for reform, and added that medical men were bribed to poison wells and streams. The non-religious displayed as great superstition in this matter as did the religious. Large bills, headed in large type " Cholera Humbug," were at that time posted on the blank walls of the streets of Glasgow. The feeling against medical men was then so intense, that some of them were mobbed, and narrowly escaped with their lives. In Paisley, considered to be the most intelligent town in Scotland, a doctor, who was working night and day for the relief of the sufferers, had his house and shop sacked, and was obliged to fly for shelter, or his life would have been sacrificed to the fury of the mob.

When we read that epidemics which broke out in the times of our forefathers, were ascribed to such absurd causes as the introduction of forks, or because the nation neglected to prosecute with sufficient vigour alleged cases of compact with the devil, we wonder at and pity their ignorance, and rejoice that we live in a more enlightened age. But the fact is, that among the mass of the people there is really no great difference between the present and the past. There is a close family likeness in this matter of superstition between now and long ago, and this state of matters will continue so long as a knowledge of physical science—that science which treats of the laws by which God is pleased to overrule and direct material things—is not made a religious duty. There are physical sins and there are moral sins, and the punishment for the

first is apparently even more direct than for the second,
for in the case of physical sins we are punished without mercy.   Through neglect of these laws, we are
continually suffering punishment, shortening and making
miserable our own lives and the lives of those dependent
upon us; and periodically judgments descend on the careless community, in the form of severe epidemics.   Any
religion which advocates practices, or teaches doctrines
inconsistent with our physical, intellectual, or moral well-
being, cannot be from God, and *vice versa;* and this is a
strong argument in favour of Christianity *as taught by its
Founder.* I wish I could say the same of the Christianity
taught by our ecclesiastics, either Protestant or Catholic.

The introduction into the heathen world of the funda-
mental truths that there is but one God, omnipotent and
omniscient, who overrules every event, that He has reveal-
ed Himself through His Son as a God of love and mercy,
and that man's duty to Him is obedience to His laws,
was a mighty step in advance of the gross conceptions of
idolatry formerly prevalent among these nations.   But
neither heathens nor Christians had for a long time any
clear idea that the overruling of God in Providence was
according to fixed laws.   Being ignorant on this point,
they ascribed to unseen supernatural agency, working in
a capricious fashion, all phenomena which appeared to
differ from, or disturb the ordinary course of events.
Upon such matters heathen and Christian ideas commingled, and thus heathen ideas and practices were incorporated with Christian ideas and practices.   Then,
when ecclesiastical councils met to determine truth, and
formulate their creeds, these combined heathen and
Christian ideas being accepted by them, became dogmas

of the Church, and henceforth those who differed from the dogmatic creed of the Church, or advocated views in advance of these confessions, were regarded as enemies of truth.   Naturally, as the Church became powerful she became more repressive, and opposed all enquiry which appeared to lead to conclusions different from those already promulgated by her, and finally, it became a capital offence to teach any other doctrines than those sanctioned by the Church.   The beliefs of the members of these councils being, as we have already seen, a mixture of heathen and Christian ideas, the Church thus became a great conservator of superstition ; and to show that this was really so, we may adduce one example :— Pope Innocent VIII. issued a Bull as follows :—" It has "come to our ears that members of both sexes do not "avoid to have intercourse with the infernal fiends, and " that, by this service, they afflict both man and beast, that " they blight the marriage bed, destroy the births of women "and the increase of cattle, they blast the corn on the " ground, the grapes of the vineyard and the fruits of the "trees, and the grass and herbs of the field."   The promulgation of this Bull is said to have produced dreadful consequences, by thousands being burned and otherwise put to death, for having intercourse with the fiends.

We regret to say such beliefs and such means of repressing free enquiry were not confined to one branch of the Christian Church.   Protestants as well as Roman Catholics, when they had the power, suppressed many of the practices of heathenism after a cruel fashion, but at the same time fostered the superstitions and Pagan beliefs which had originated these practices, and punished those who protested against these beliefs.   The same method of procedure is in operation at the present day. Never-theless, the introduction of Christianity into the heathen world made a wonderful revolution in their religious practices as well as in their beliefs. Their idols and the symbols of their divinities were abolished, along with the sacrifices offered to these. Their great festivals, at which human sacrifices were offered and abominable practices committed, were so modified as to be stripped of their immorality and cruelty, and while being retained—re-tained because they could not be utterly abolished—they were Christianized,—that is, a Christian colouring was given to them,—and they became Church festivals or holydays,—a subject I will treat more fully of in another chapter.

It is not, as I have already said, my intention to trace the gradual development of our modern idea of Provi-dence, our ascription of universal government, of all di-rection of the phenomena of nature and of life to the one only omnipotent, omniscient, and omnipresent God, but rather to place before the reader the practices and beliefs which prevailed in this country during the early years of the present century. And from this survey we shall dis-cover what a mass of old Pagan ideas still survived and influenced the minds and practice of the people,—how they yet clung to the notion that many of the pheno-mena of nature and life were under the control of super-natural agents, although they did not regard these agents, as what in olden times they were considered to be—di-vinities, but believed them to be a class of beings living upon or within the earth, and endowed by the devil with supernatural powers.

In the northern sagas, and in the old ballads and saintly

legends of the Middle Ages—supernatural agents who played a prominent part—there are giants of enormous size and little dwarfs who can make themselves invisible, and do all sorts of good to their favourites, and harm to their enemies. We are also introduced there to dragons and other monsters which have human understandings, and, guided by a wicked spirit, could do great mischief. Such beings took the place of the ancient divinities, and in many cases when the hero or saint is in great straits, in combat with these evil spirits or fiends, Jesus Christ comes to their assistance. One instance will exemplify this :

> " O'er him stood the foul fiends,
> And with their clubs of steel,
> Struck him o'er the helmit
> That in deadly swound he fell.
> But God his sorrow saw,
> To the fiends his Son he sent ;
> From the earth they vanished
> With howling and lament.
> The Christian hero thanked his God,
> From the ground he rose with speed,
> Joyfully he sheathed his sword,
> And mounted on his steed."
> *Illustrations of " Northern Antiquities."*

By the beginning of this century these ideas of the *personel* of supernatural agencies had become slightly modified in this country at least, giants and dragons having given way to fairies, brownies, elves, witches, etc. The Rev. Mr. Kirk, of Aberfeldy, published a work descriptive of these supernatural beings. He says they are a kind of astral spirits between angels and humanity, being like men and women in appearance, and similar in many of their habits; some of them, however, are double. They marry and have children, for which they keep nurses; have deaths and burials amongst them, and they can make themselves visible or invisible at pleasure. They live in subterranean habitations, and in an invisible condition attend very constantly on men. They are very fond of human children and pretty women, both of which they will steal if not protected by some superior influence. Women in childbed stand in danger of being taken, but if a piece of cold iron be kept in the bed in which they lie, the spirits won't come near. Children are in greater danger of being stolen before baptism than after. They sometimes, to supply their own needs, spirit away the milk from cows, but more frequently they transfer the milk to the cows of some person who stands high in their favour. This they do by making themselves invisible, and silently milking and removing the milk in invisible vessels. When people offend them they shoot flint-tipped arrows, and by this means kill either the persons who have offended them or their cattle. They cause these arrows to strike the most vital part, but the stroke does not visibly break the skin, only a *blae* mark is the result visible on the body after death. These flint arrow-heads are occasionally found, and the possession of one of these will protect the possessor against the power of these astral beings, and at the same time enable him or her to cure disease in cattle and women. These flints were often sewed into the dresses of children to protect them from the Evil-eye. There were many other means of protection against the power of these beings, which we shall have occasion to refer to again. There is one method, however, which may be mentioned now. If, when a calf is born, its mouth be smeared with a balsam of dung, before it is allowed to suck, the fairies cannot milk that cow. Those taken to fairyland lose the power of calculating the lapse of time, although they are not unconscious of what is going on around them. Those spirited away to fairyland may be recovered by their friends or relatives, by performing certain formula, or—and this was often the method resorted to—by out-witting the fairies, getting possession of their stolen friends, and then doing or saying something which fairies cannot bear, upon which they are forced to depart, leaving the recovered party behind them.

The following information concerning the government, &c., of fairyland, is taken from Aytoun :—The queen of fairyland was a kind of feudatory sovereign under Satan, to whom she was obliged to pay *kave*, or tithe in kind ; and, as her own fairy subjects strongly objected to trans-fer their allegiance, the quota was usually made up in children who had been stolen before the rite of baptism had been administered to them. This belief was at one time universal throughout all Scotland, and was still pre-valent at the beginning of this century. Charms were quite commonly employed to defend houses from the inroads of the fairies before the infants were baptised ; but even baptism did not always protect the baby from being stolen. During the period of infancy, the mother required to be ever watchful; but the risks were espe-cially great before baptism. It is difficult to define exactly the power which the queen of elfland had, for besides carrying off Thomas the Rhymer, she was sup-posed to have carried off no less a personage than James IV. from the field of Flodden, and to have detained him in her enchanted country. There was also a king of

elfland. From the accounts extracted from or volunteered by witches, &c., preserved to us in justiciary and
presbyterial records, he appears to have been a peace-
able, luxurious, indolent personage, who entrusted the
whole business of his kingdom, including the recruiting
department, to his wife. We get a glimpse of both their
majesties in the confessions of Isabella Gowdie, in
Aulderne, a parish in Nairnshire, who was indicted for
witchcraft in 1662. She said—"I was in Downie Hills,
and got meat there from the queen of the fairies, more
than I could eat. · The queen is brawly clothed in white
linen, and in white and brown cloth; and the king is a
braw man, well-favoured, and broad-faced. There were
plenty of elf bulls rowting and skoyling up and down,
and affrighted me." Mr. Kirk says ,"that in fairyland
they have also books of various kinds—history, travels,
novels, and plays—but no sermons, no Bible, nor any
book of a religious kind." Every reader of Hogg's
Queen's Wake knows the beautiful legend of the abduc-
tion of "Bonny Kilmeny"; but in Dr. Jamieson's
Illustrations of Northern Antiquities we have found
amongst these heroic and romantic ballads another
legend more fully descriptive of fairyland. In this
legend, a young lady is carried away to fairyland, and
recovered, by her brother :—

> " King Arthur's sons o' merry Carlisle
>   Were playing at the ba',
> And there was their sister, burd Ellen,
>   I' the midst, amang them a'.
> Child Rowland kicked it wi' his foot,
> · And keppit it wi' his knee ;
> And aye as he played, out o'er them a',
>   O'er the kirk he gar'd it flee.

> Burd Ellen round about the aisle
>   To seek the ba' has gane;
> But she bade lang, and ay langer,
>   And she came na back again.
> They sought her east, they sought her west,
>   They sought her up and down,
> And wae were the hearts in merry Carlisle,
>   For she was nae gait found."

Merlin, the warlock, being consulted, told them that burd Ellen was taken away by the fairies, and that it would be a dangerous task to recover her if they were not well instructed how to proceed. The instructions which Merlin gave were, that whoever undertook the quest for her should, after entering elfland, kill every person he met till he reached the royal apartments, and taste neither meat nor drink offered to them, for by doing otherwise they would come under the fairy spell, and never again get back to earth. Two of her brothers undertook the journey, but disobeyed the instructions of the warlock, and were retained in elfland. Child Rowland, her youngest brother, then arming himself with his father's claymore, *excalibar*—that never struck in vain—set out on the dangerous quest. Strictly observing the warlock's instructions, after asking his way to the king of elfland's castle of every servant he met, he, in accordance with these instructions, when he had received the desired information, slew the servant. The last fairy functionary he met was the hen-wife, who told him to go on a little further till he came to a round green hill surrounded with rings from the bottom to the top, then go round it *widershins* (contrary to the sun) and every time he made the circuit, say—"Open door, open door, and let me come in," and on the third repetition of this incantation they would open, and he might then go in. Having received this information, he fulfilled his instructions, and slew the hen-wife. Then proceeding as directed, he soon reached the green hill, and made the circuit of it three times, repeating the words before mentioned. On the third repetition of the words the door opened, and he went in, the door closing behind him. "He proceeded through a long passage, where the air was soft and agreeably warm, like a May evening, as is all the air in elf-land. The light was a sort of twilight or gloaming; but there were neither windows nor candles, and he knew not whence it came if it was not from the walls and roof, which were rough and arched like a grotto, and composed of a clear transparent rock incrusted with *sheep's silver*, and spar and various bright stones." At last he came to two lofty folding doors which stood ajar. Passing through these doors, he entered a large and spacious hall, the richness and brilliance of which was beyond description. It seemed to extend throughout the whole length and breadth of the hill. The superb Gothic pillars by which the roof was supported were so large and lofty, that the pillars of the "Chaury Kirk or of the Pluscardin Abbey are no more to be compared to them than the Knock of Alves is to be compared to Balrimes or Ben-a-chi." They were of gold and silver, and were fretted like the west window of the Chaury Kirk (Elgin Cathedral), with wreaths of flowers, composed of diamonds and precious stones of all manner of beautiful colours. The key stones of the arches, instead of being escutcheoned, were ornamented also with clusters of diamonds in brilliant devices.

From the middle of the roof, where the arches met, was hung, suspended by a gold chain, an immense lamp of one hollowed pearl, and perfectly transparent, in the centre of which was a large carbuncle, which, by the power of magic, turned round continually, and shed throughout all the hall a clear mild light like that of the setting sun. But the hall was so large, and these dazzling objects so far removed, that their blended radiance cast no more than a pleasing mellow lustre around, and excited no other than agreeable sensations in the eyes of Child Rowland. The furniture of the hall was suitable to its architecture; and at the further end, under a splendid canopy, sitting on a gorgeous sofa of velvet, silk and gold, and "kembing her yellow hair wi' a silver kemb,"

> "Was his sister Burd Ellen.
> She stood up him before,
> God rue or thee poor luckless fode (man),
> What hast thou to do here?
> And hear ye this my youngest brother,
> Why badena ye at hame?
> Had ye a hunder and thousand lives
> Ye canna brook ane o' them.
> And sit thou down; and wae, oh wae!
> That ever thou was born,
> For came the King o' Elfland in,
> Thy leccam (body) is forlorn."

After a long conversation with his sister, the two folding doors were burst open with tremendous violence, and in came the King of Elfland, shouting—

> "With *fi, fe, fa*, and *fum*,
> I smell the blood of a Christian man,
> Be he dead, be he living, with my brand
> I'll clash his harns frae his harn pan."

Child Rowland drew his good claymore (*excalibar*) that never struck in vain. A furious combat ensued, and the king was defeated; but Child Rowland spared his life on condition that he would free his sister, Burd Ellen, and his two brothers, who were lying in a trance in a corner of the hall. The king then produced a small crystal phial containing a bright red liquor, with which he anointed the lips, nostrils, ears and finger tips of the two brothers, who thereupon awoke as from a profound sleep, and all four returned in triumph to "merry Carlisle." The Rev. Mr. Kirk's descriptions of the subterranean homes of the fairies and of their social habits are just the counterparts of the fairyland of this beautiful ballad legend. There can be little doubt that such beliefs are but survivals in altered form of what were in still more ancient times religious tenets. What were formerly divinities have given place to the more lowly fairies, brownies, &c., and from the position of Pagan gods they have, through the opposing influence of Christianity, been removed to the other side, and became servants of the devil, actively opposing the kingdom of Christ. Some have supposed that the fairies may have originally been considered to be descendants of the Druids, for some reason consigned to inhabit subterranean caves under green hills in wild and lonely glens. Others have identified them with the fallen angels. One thing is certain, that the notion that there exists supernatural men, women, and animals who inhabit subterranean and submarine regions, and yet can indulge in intercourse with the human race, is of very great antiquity, and widely spread, existing in Arabia, Persia, India, Thibet, among the Tartars, Swedes, Norwegians,

British, and also among the savage tribes of Africa. In the west of Scotland there was a class of fairies who acted a friendly part towards their human neighbours, helping the weak or ill-used, and generally busying themselves with acts of kindness; these were called "brownies." The fairies proper were a merry race, full of devilment, and malicious, tricky, and troublesome, and the cause of much annoyance and fear among the people. Besides these supernatural. beings—brownies, fairies, &c.—there existed a belief in persons who were possessed of supernatural powers—magicians, sorcerers, &c. About the Reformation period, these persons were considered to be in the actual service of the devil, who was then thought to be raising a more determined opposition than ever to the spread of the kingdom of God, and adopting the insidious means of enlisting men and women into his service by conferring upon them supernatural powers; so that by this contract they were bound to do mischief to all good Christian people ; and the more mischief they could do the greater would be the favours they received from their master. This belief was not confined to the ignorant, but was equally accepted by the educated and by the Church. Measures were taken to frustrate the devil, and the faithful were recommended to make search for those who had compacted with his Satanic Majesty, and laws were enacted for the punishment of the compacters when found. The faithful, under the belief that they were fighting the battle of the Lord, brought numbers of poor wretches to trial, many of whom, strangely enough, believed themselves guilty of the crime imputed to them. After trial and conviction, they were put to death. The belief that the devil could and did invest men and women with supernatural powers affected all social relations, for everything strange and unaccountable—and, in a non-scientific age, we can readily conceive how almost everything would be brought into this category—was ascribed to this cause, and each suspected his or her neighbour; even the truest friendship was sometimes broken through this suspicion. The laws against witchcraft in this country were abrogated last century, but the abrogation of the law could not be expected to work any sudden change in the belief of the people; at most, the alteration only paved the way for the gradual departure of the superstition, and since the abrogation of the law the belief has been decaying, but still in many parts of the country it lingers on till the present time, instances of which appear every now and again in the newspapers of the day.

CHAPTER II.

HEN writing of fairies I noticed,—but as it is connected with birth, I may here mention it again,—a practice common in some localities of placing in the bed where lay an expectant mother, a piece of cold iron to scare the fairies, and prevent them from spiriting away mother and child to elfland. An instance of this spiriting away at the time of child-bearing is said to have occurred in Arran within these fifty years. It is given by a correspondent in *Long Ago*:—"There was a woman near " Pladda, newly delivered, who was carried away, and on " a certain night her wraith stood before her husband " telling him that the yearly riding was at hand, and that " she, with all the rout, should ride by his house at such " an hour, on such a night; that he must await her coming, " and throw over her her wedding gown, and so she " should be rescued from her tyrants. With that she " vanished. And the time came, with the jingling of " bridles and the tramping of horses outside the cottage ; " but this man, feeble-hearted, had summoned his neigh- " bours to bear him company, who held him, and would " not suffer him to go out. So there arose a bitter cry " and a great clamour, and then all was still; but in the " morning, roof and wall were dashed with blood, and the

"sorrowful wife was no more seen upon earth. This,"
says the writer, "is not a tale from an old ballad, it
"is the narrative of what was told not fifty years ago."

Immediately after birth, the newly-born child was
bathed in salted water, and made to taste of it three
times. This, by some, was considered a specific against
the influence of the evil eye ; but doctors differ, and so
among other people and in other localities different
specifics were employed. I quote the following from
Ross' Helenore :—

> "Gryte was the care and tut'ry that was ha'en,
> Baith night and day about the bonny weeane :
> The jizzen-bed, wi' rantry leaves was sain'd,
> And sic like things as the auld grannies kend ;
> Jean's paps wi' saut and water washen clean,
> Reed that her milk gat wrang, fan it was green ;
> Neist the first hippen to the green was flung,
> And there at seelfu' words, baith said and sung :
> A clear brunt coal wi' the het tangs was ta'en,
> Frae out the ingle-mids fu' clear and clean,
> And throu' the cosey-belly letten fa',
> For fear the weeane should be ta'en awa'."

Before baptism the child was more liable to be
influenced by the evil eye than after that ceremony
had been performed, consequently before that rite
had been administered the greatest precautions were
taken, the baby during this time being kept as much
as possible in the room in which it was born, and
only when absolutely necessary, carried out of it,
and then under the careful guardianship of a relative,
or of the mid-wife, who was professionally skilled in all
the requisites of safety. Baptism was therefore administered as early as possible after birth. Another reason
for the speedy administration of this rite was that, should

the baby die before being baptised, its future was not doubtful. Often on calm nights, those who had ears to hear heard the wailing of the spirits of unchristened bairns among the trees and dells. I have known of an instance in which the baby was born on a Saturday, and carried two miles to church next day, rather than risk a week's delay. It was rare for working people to bring the minister to the house. Another superstitious notion in connection with baptism was that until that rite was performed, it was unlucky to name the child by any name. When, before the child had been christened, any one asked the name of the baby, the answer generally was, "It has not been out yet." Let it be remembered that these notions were entertained by people who were not Romanists, but Protestants, and therefore did not profess to believe in the saving efficacy of baptism,—who could answer every question in the Shorter Catechism, and repeat the Creed, and Ten Commandments, to the satisfaction of elder and minister. But all this verbal acquaintance with dogma was powerless to eradicate, even, we may venture to say, from the minds of elder and minister, the deeply-rooted fibres of ancient superstition, which had been long crystallised in the Roman Catholic Church, and could not be easily forgot in that of the Protestant.

When a child was taken from its mother and carried outside the bedroom for the first time after its birth, it was lucky to take it up stairs, and unlucky to take it down stairs. If there were no stairs in the house, the person who carried it generally ascended three steps of a ladder or temporary erection, and this, it was supposed, would bring prosperity to the child.

A child born with a caul—a thin membrane covering the head of some children at birth—would, if spared, prove a notable person. The carrying of a caul on board ship was believed to prevent shipwreck, and masters of vessels paid a high price for them. I have seen an advertisement for such in a local paper.

When baby was being carried to church to be baptised, it was of importance that the woman appointed to this post should be known to be lucky. Then she took with her a parcel of bread and cheese, which she gave to the first person she met. This represented a gift from the baby—a very ancient custom. Again, it was of importance that the person who received this gift should be lucky—should have lucky marks upon their person. Forecasts were made from such facts as the following concerning the recipient of the gift :—Was this person male or female, deformed, disfigured, plain-soled, etc. If the party accepted the gift willingly, tasted it, and returned a few steps with the baptismal party, this was a good sign ; if they asked to look at the baby, and blessed it, this was still more favourable : but should this person refuse the gift, nor taste it, nor turn back, this was tantamount to wishing evil to the child, and should any serious calamity befal the child, even years after, it was connected with this circumstance, and the party who had refused the baptismal gift was blamed for the evil which had befallen the child. It was also a common belief that if, as was frequently the case, there were several babies, male and female, awaiting baptism together, and the males were baptised before the females, all was well ; but if, by mistake, a female should be christened before a male, the characters of the pair would be reversed—the female would grow up with a masculine character, and would have a beard, whereas the male would display a feminine disposition and be beardless. I have known where such a mistake has produced real anxiety and regret in the minds of the parents. We have seen that it was not until after baptism that the child was allowed out of the room in which it was born, except under the skilful guardianship of a relative or the midwife ; but, further than this, it was not considered safe or proper to carry it into any neighbour's house until the mother took it herself, and this it was unlucky even for her to do until she had been to church. Indeed, few mothers would enter any house until they had been to the house of God. After this had been accomplished, however, she visited with the baby freely. In visiting any house with baby for the first time, it was incumbent on the person whom they were visiting to put a little salt or sugar into baby's mouth, and wish it well : the omission of this was regarded as a very unlucky omen for the baby. Here we may note the survival of a very ancient symbolic practice in this gift of salt. Salt was symbolical of favour or good will, and covenants of friendship in very early times were ratified with this gift; sugar, as in this instance, is no doubt a modern substitute for salt. Among Jews, Greeks, and Romans, as well as among less civilised nations, salt was used in their sacrifices as emblematic of fidelity, and for some reason or other it also came to be regarded as a charm against evil fascinations. By Roman Catholics in the middle ages, salt was used to protect children from evil influences before they had received the sacrament of baptism. This practice is referred to in many of the old

E

"nurse to pray for me or mine; good Jupiter, be sure to
"refuse her, though she may have put on white for the
"occasion."

The Romans used to hang red coral round the necks
of their children to save them from falling-sickness, sor-
cery, charms, and poison. In this country coral beads
were hung round the necks of babies, and are still used
in country districts to protect them from an evil eye.
Coral bells are used at present. The practice was originated by the Roman Catholics to frighten away evil
spirits.

I have quite a vivid remembrance of being myself believed to be the unhappy victim of an evil eye. I had
taken what was called a *dwining*, which baffled all
ordinary experience; and, therefore, it was surmised that
I had got "a blink of an ill e'e." To remove this evil
influence, I was subjected to the following operation,
which was prescribed and superintended by a neighbour "skilly" in such matters :—A sixpence was borrowed
from a neighbour, a good fire was kept burning in the
grate, the door was locked, and I was placed upon a
chair in front of the fire. The operator, an old woman,
took a tablespoon and filled it with water. With the
sixpence she then lifted as much salt as it could carry,
and both were put into the water in the spoon. The
water was then stirred with the forefinger till the salt was
dissolved. Then the soles of my feet and the palms of
my hands were bathed with this solution thrice, and
after these bathings I was made to taste the solution three
times. The operator then drew her wet forefinger across
my brow,—called *scoring aboon the breath*. The remaining contents of the spoon she then cast right over

the fire, into the hinder part of the fire, saying as she did so, "*Guid preserve frae a' skaith.*" These were the first words permitted to be spoken during the operation. I was then put in bed, and, in attestation of the efficacy of the charm, recovered. To my knowledge this operation has been performed within these 40 years, and probably in many outlying country places it is still practised. The origin of this superstition is probably to be found in ancient fire worship. The great blazing fire was evidently an important element in the transaction ; nor was this a solitary instance in which regard was paid to fire. I remember being taught that it was unlucky to spit into the fire, some evil being likely shortly after to befall those who did so. Crumbs left upon the table after a meal were carefully gathered and put into the fire. The cuttings from the nails and hair were also put into the fire. These freaks certainly look like survivals of fire worship.

The influence of those possessing the evil eye was not confined to children, but might affect adults, and also goods and cattle. But for the bane there was provided the antidote. One effective method of checking the evil influence was by *scoring aboon the breath.* In my case, as I was the victim, *scoring* with a wet finger was sufficient ; but the suspected possessor of the evil eye was more roughly treated, *scoring* in this case being effected with some sharp instrument so as to draw blood. I have never seen this done, but some fifty years ago an instance occurred in my native village. A child belonging to a poor woman in this village was taken ill and had convulsive fits, which were thought to be due to the influence of the evil eye. An old woman in the

neighbourhood, whose temper was not of the sweetest,
was suspected.   She was first of all invited to come and
see the child in the hope that sympathy might change
the influence she was supposed to be exerting ; but as
the old woman appeared quite callous to the sufferings
of the child, the mother, as the old woman was leaving the
house, scratched her with her nails across the brow, and
drew blood.   This circumstance raised quite a sensation
in the village.   Whether the child recovered after this
operation I do not remember.   Many other instances of
the existence of this superstitious practice in Scotland
within the present century might be presented, but I content myself with quoting one which was related in a letter
to the *Glasgow Weekly Herald*, under the signature F. A. :
—" I knew of one case of the kind in Wigtownshire, in
" the south of Scotland, about the year 1825, as near as
" I can mind.   I knew all parties very well.   A farmer
" had some cattle which died, and there was an old
" woman living about a mile from the farm who was
" counted no very canny.   She was heard to say that
" there would be mair o' them wad gang the same way.
" So one day, soon after, as the old woman was passing
" the farmhouse, one of the sons took hold of her and
" got her head under his arm, and cut her across the
" forehead.   By the way, the proper thing to be cut with
" is a nail out of a horse-shoe.   He was prosecuted and
" got imprisonment for it."

This style of antidote against the influence of an evil
eye was common in England within the century, as the
following, which is also taken from a letter which appeared
in the same journal, seems to show :—"Drawing blood from
" above the mouth of the person suspected is the

"favourite antidote in the neighbourhood of Burn-
"ley; and in the district of Craven, a few miles
"within the borders of Yorkshire, a person who was ill-
"disposed towards his neighbours is believed to have
"slain a pear-tree which grew opposite his house by
"directing towards it 'the first morning glances' of his
"evil eye. Spitting three times in the person's face;
"turning a live coal on the fire; and exclaiming, 'The
"Lord be with us,' are other means of averting its in-
"fluence."

We must not, however, pursue this digression further,
but return to our proper subject. It was not necessary that
the person possessed of the evil eye, and desirous of in-
flicting evil upon a child, should see the child. All that
was necessary was that the person with the evil eye should
get possession of something which had belonged to the
child, such as a fragment of clothing, a toy, hair, or nail
parings. I may note here that it was not considered
lucky to pare the nails of a child under one year old,
and when the operation was performed the mother was
careful to collect every scrap of the cutting, and burn
them. It was considered a great offence for any person,
other than the mother or near relation, in whom every
confidence could be placed, to cut a baby's nails; if
some forward officious person should do this, and baby
afterwards be taken ill, this would give rise to grave sus-
picions of evil influence being at work. The same remarks apply to the cutting of a baby's hair. I have seen
the door locked during hair-cutting, and the floor swept
afterwards, and the sweepings burned, lest perchance any
hairs might remain, and be picked up by an enemy. Dr.
Livingstone, in his book on the Zambesi, mentions the

existence of a similar practice among some African tribes.
"They carefully collect and afterwards burn or bury the
hair, lest any of it fall into the hands of a witch." Mr.
Munter mentions that the same practice is common
amongst the Patagonians, and the practice extends to
adults. He says that after bathing, which they do every
morning, "the men's hair is dressed by their wives,
" daughters, or sweethearts, who take the greatest care to
" burn the hairs that may be brushed out, as they fully
" believe that spells may be wrought by evil-intentioned
" persons who can obtain a piece of their hair. From the
" same idea, after cutting their nails the parings are care-
" fully committed to the flames."

Besides this danger—this blighting influence of the evil
eye which environed the years of childhood—there was
also this other danger, already mentioned, that of being
spirited away by fairies. The danger from this source
was greater when the baby was pretty, and what fond
mother did not consider her baby pretty? Early in the
century, a labourer's wife living a few miles west of Glasgow, became the mother of a very pretty baby. All who
saw it were charmed with its beauty, and it was as good as
it was bonnie. The neighbours often urged on the mother
the necessity of carefulness, and advised her to adopt
such methods as were, to their minds, well-attested safe-
guards for the preservation of children from fairy influence
and an evil eye. She was instructed never to leave the
child without placing near it an open Bible. One unhappy
day the mother went out for a short time, leaving the
baby in its cradle, but she forgot or neglected to place
the open Bible near the child as directed. When she
returned baby was crying, and could by no means be

quieted, and the mother observed several blue marks upon its person, as if it had been pinched. From that day it became a perfect plague ; no amount of food or drink would satisfy it, and yet withal it became lean. The *girn*, my informant said, was never out its face, and it *yammered* on night and day. One day an old highland woman having seen the child, and inspected it carefully, affirmed that it was a fairy child. She went the length of offering to put the matter to the test, and this is how she tested it. She put the poker in the fire, and hung a pot over the fire wherein were put certain ingredients, an incantation being said as each new ingredient was stirred into the pot. The child was quiet during these opera-tions, and watched like a grown person all that was being done, even rising upon its elbow to look. When the operations were completed, the old woman took the poker out of the fire, and carrying it red hot over to the cradle, was about to burn the sign of the cross on the baby's brow, when the child sprung suddenly up, knocked the old woman down and disappeared up the *lum* (chimney,) filling the house with smoke, and leaving behind it a strong smell of brimstone. When the smoke cleared away, the true baby was found in the cradle sleeping as if it never had been taken away. Another case was related to me as having occurred in the same neighbourhood, but in this instance the theft was not discovered until after the death of the child. The surreptitious or false baby, having apparently died, was buried ; but suspicion having been raised, the grave was opened and the coffin examined, when there was found in it, not a corpse, but a wooden figure. The late Mr. Rust, in his *Druidism Ex-humed*, states that this superstition is common in the

North of Scotland, and adds that it is also believed that if
the theft be discovered before the apparent death of the
changling, there are means whereby the fairies may be
propitiated and induced to restore the real baby.   One
of these methods is the following:—The parents or friends
of the stolen baby must take the fairy child to some
known haunt of the fairies, generally some spot where
peculiar *soughing* sounds are heard, where there are remains of some ancient cairn or stone circle, or some green
mound or shady dell, and lay the child down there, repeating certain incantations.   They must also place beside it a quantity of bread, butter, milk, cheese, eggs, and
flesh of fowl, then retire to a distance and wait for an
hour or two, or until after midnight.   If on going back
to where the child was laid they find that the offerings
have disappeared, it is held as evidence that the fairies
have been satisfied, and that the human child is returned.   The baby is then carried home, and great rejoicing
made.   Mr. Rust states that he knew a woman who,
when a baby, had been stolen away, but was returned by
this means.

CHAPTER III.

MARRIAGE.

THE next very important event in man's life is marriage, and naturally, therefore, to this event there attached a multitude of superstitious notions and practices, many of which, indeed, do still exist. The time when marriage took place was of considerable importance. One very prevalent superstition, common alike to all classes in the community, and whose force is not yet spent, was the belief that it was unlucky to marry in the month of May. The aversion to marrying in May finds expression in the very ancient and well-known proverb, "Marry in May, rue for aye," and thousands still avoid marrying in this month who can render no more solid reason for their aversion than the authority of this old proverb. But in former times there were reasons given, varying, however, in different localities. Some of the reasons given were the following :—That parties so marrying would be childless, or, if they had children, that the first-born would be an idiot, or have some physical deformity; or that the married couple would not lead a happy life, and would soon tire of each other's society. The origin of this superstition is to be found in ancient heathen religious beliefs and practices. We have already noticed the ancient belief that the spirits of dead ancestors haunted the living, and I have given a formula whereby a single person could exorcise the ghosts of his departed relatives, and I have also mentioned that national festivals to propitiate the spirits of the dead were appointed by some nations. Now, we find that among the Romans this national festival was held during the month of May, and during its continuance all other forms of worship were suspended, and the temples shut; and further, for any couple to contract marriage during this season was held to be a daring of the Fates which few were found hardy enough to venture. Ovid says—

> " Pause while we keep these rites, ye widowed dames,
> The marriage time a purer season claims ;
> Pause, ye fond mothers, braid not yet her hair,
> Nor the ripe virgin for her lord prepare.
> O, light not, Hymen, now your joyous fires,
> Another torch nor yours the tomb requires !
> Close all the temples on these mourning days,
> And dim each altar's spicy, steaming blaze ;
> For now around us roams a spectred brood,
> Craving and keen, and snuffing mortal food :
> They feast and revel, nor depart again,
> Till to the month but ten days more remain."

Superstitions of this sort linger much longer in the country than in towns, and the larger the town the more speedily do they die out ; but, judging from the statistics of late years, this superstition has still a firm hold of the inhabitants of Glasgow, the second city of the Empire. During the year 1874 the marriages in May were only 204, against 703 in June; but as the removal term occurs at the end of May, that must materially affect the relations, in this respect, between May and June, and accounts, in part, for the great excess of marriages in June.

But if the average of the eleven months, excluding May, be taken, then during that year there was a monthly average of 441, against 204 in May—being rather more than double. For the ten years preceding 1874, the average of the eleven months was 388, against 203 in May. As if to compensate for the restraint put upon the people in May, *Juno*, the wife of Jupiter, after whom June was named, and whose influence was paramount during that month, took special guardianship over births and marriages; hence June was a lucky month to be born in or get married in, and thus June is known as the marrying month. Here, again, our registers show that the number of marriages are in June nearly double the average of the other months, excluding May and June. The average during the ten years is, for the ten months, 375 per month, whilst the average for June is 598. It may be noticed in passing that, in Glasgow, January and July stand as high as June, owing, doubtless, to the holidays which occur during these two months making marriage at those times more convenient for the working classes.

There were many marriage observances of a religious or superstitious character practised in ancient Rome which were quite common among us within this century, especially in the country districts, but which now are either extinct or fast dying out. When a Roman girl was betrothed, she received from her intended a ring which she wore as evidence of her betrothal. When betrothed she laid aside her girlish or maiden dress,— some parts of which were offered as a sacrifice to the household gods,—and she was then clothed in the dress of a wife, and secluded from her former

companions, and put under training for her new
duties. When the time drew near for the consum-
mation of the ceremony, it became an important
consideration to fix upon a lucky day and hour for the
knot to be tied. With this object astrologers, sooth-
sayers, and others of that class were consulted, who, by
certain divinations ascertained the most auspicious
time for the union to take place in. When the day
arrived every occurrence was watched for omens. A crow
or turtle dove appearing near was a good omen: for these
birds symbolized conjugal fidelity. The ceremony was
begun by sacrificing a sheep to Juno, the fleece being
spread upon two chairs on which the bride and bridegroom sat: then a prayer was said over them. The
young wife, carrying a distaff and spindle filled with
wool, was conducted to her house, a cake, baked by the
vestal virgins, being carried before her. The threshold
of the house was disenchanted by charms, and by an-
nointing it with certain unctuous perfumes; but as it
was considered unlucky for the new-made wife to tread
upon the threshold on first entering her house, she was
lifted over it and seated upon a piece of wool, a symbol
of domestic industry. The keys of the house were then
put into her hand, and the cake was divided among the
guests. The first work of the young wife was to spin
new garments for her husband. It will be seen that
many of these practices were mixed up with superstitious
notions, many of which were prevalent in this country
sixty years ago, and some of which still remain in country
districts. Sixty years ago when a young woman became
a bride, she in a great measure secluded herself from
society, and mixed but little even with her companions,

and on no account would she show herself at church until after her marriage, as that was considered very un-lucky. The evening before the marriage her presents and outfit were conveyed to her future home under the superintendence of the best maid (bridesmaid), who carried with her a certain domestic utensil filled with salt, which was the first article of the bride's furnishing taken into the house. A portion of the salt was sprinkled over the floor as a protection against an evil eye. The house being set in order, the best maid returned to the bride's house where a company of the bride's companions were met, and then occurred the ceremony of washing the bride's feet. This was generally the occasion of much mirth. And this was in all probability a survival of an old Scandinavian custom under which the Norse bride was conducted by her maiden friends to undergo a bath, called the bride's bath, a sort of religious purification. On the marriage day, every trifling circumstance which would have passed without notice at other times was noted and scanned for omens of good or evil. If the morning was clear and shining, this betokened a happy cheerful life ; if dull and raining, the contrary result might be anticipated. I have known the following incidents cause grave concern about the future prospects of the young couple:—A clot of soot coming down the chimney and spoiling the breakfast; the bride accidentally breaking a dish ; a bird sitting on the window sill chirping for some time ; the bird in the cage dying that morning ; a dog howling, and the postman forgetting to deliver a letter to the bride until he was a good way off, and had to return. Some of these were defined for good, but most of them were evil omens.

and took her away by force from her home, or he gained
the right to make her his bride by success in battle with
his opponents. Often, however, one who was no hero
might gain the consent of the parents to his marriage
with their daughter, she having little or no voice in the
matter; and when she and her friends were on their way
to the church, some heroic but unapproved admirer, determined to win her by force of arms, having collected
his followers and friends who were ever ready for a fight,
would fall upon the marriage cortege, and carry off the
bride. Under those circumstances there was often great
anxiety on the part of both the groom's and bride's
relations, who remained at home when they had reason
to apprehend that such attack might be made, and so,
whenever the marriage ceremony was over, some of the
company hasted home with the glad news; but commonly
youths stationed themselves at the church-door, ready to
run the moment the ceremony was over, and whether on
foot or horseback, the race became an exciting one. He
who first brought the good news received as a reward a
bowl of brose, and such brose as was made in those days
for this occasion was an acceptable prize. Although the
necessity for running ceased, the sport occasioned by
these contentions was too good and exciting to be readily
given up, but it came to be confined to those who were at
the wedding, and many young men looked forward
eagerly to taking part in the sport. The prize which
originally was brose, came to be changed to something
more congenial to the tastes and usages of the times, viz.,
a bottle of whiskey. In this way, I think, we may account
for the custom of "running the braize." It has been
mentioned already that the best man went with the bride

to the minister. His duty it was to take charge of the bride and hand her over to the bridegroom, a duty now performed by the bride's father, and in this now obsolete custom, I think we may find a still further proof that the management and customs of the marriage procession were founded upon the old practice of wife-capture. The best man is evidently just the bridegroom's friend, who, in the absence of the bridegroom, undertakes to protect the bride against a raid until she reaches the church, when he hands her over to his friend the bridegroom.

To meet a funeral either in going to or coming from marriage was very unlucky. If the funeral was that of a female, the young wife would not live long; if a male, the bridegroom would die soon.

After partaking of the *braize's* hospitality,—for the bottle of whiskey was his by right,—the wedding party proceeded to the house of the young couple, and in some parts of Scotland, at the beginning of the century, the young wife was lifted over the threshold, or first step of the door, lest any witchcraft or *ill e'e* should be cast upon and influence her. Just at the entering of the house, the young man's mother broke a cake of bread, prepared for the occasion, over the young wife's head. She was then led to the hearth, and the poker and tongs —in some places the broom also—were put into her hands, as symbols of her office and duty. After this, her mother-in-law handed her the keys of the house and furniture, thus transferring the mother's rights over her son to his wife. Again the glass went round, and each guest drank and wished happiness to the young pair. The cake which was broken over the young wife's head was now gathered and distributed among the unmarried female guests, and by them retained to be placed under their pillows, so that they might dream of their future husbands. This is a custom still practised, but what is now the bridescake is not a cake broken over the bride's head, but a larger and more elaborately-prepared article, which is cut up and distributed immediately after the marriage ceremony. Young girls still put a piece of it under their pillows in order to obtain prophetic dreams. In some cases, this is done by a friend writing the names of three young men on a piece of paper, and the cake, wrapped in it, is put under the pillow for three nights in succession before it is opened. Should the owners of the cake have dreamed of one of the three young men therein written, it is regarded as a sure proof that he is to be her future husband. After drinking to the health and happiness of the young couple, the wedding party then went to the house of the bridegroom's father where they partook of supper, generally a very substantial meal; and this being finished, the young people of the party became restless for a change of amusement, and generally all then repaired to some hall or barn, and there spent the night in dancing. It was the custom for the young couple, with their respective parents and the best man and the best maid, to lead off by dancing the first reel. Should the young couple happen to have either brothers or sisters older than themselves, but unmarried, these unfortunate brethren danced the first reel without their shoes. Probably this has its origin in the old Jewish custom of giving up the shoe or sandal when the right or priority passed from one to another. For an instance of this see Ruth iv. 7. Having danced till far on in the morning of next day, the young couple were then conducted home. The young wife, assisted by her female friends, undressed and got to bed, then the young man was sent into bed by his friends, and then all the marriage party entered the bedroom, when the young wife took one of her stockings, which had been put in bed with her, and threw it among the company. The person who got this was to be the first married. The best man then handed round the glass, and when all had again drank to the young couple, the company retired. This custom was termed *the bedding*, and was regarded as a ceremony necessary to the completion of the marriage; and there can be little doubt that it is a survival of a very ancient ceremony of the same family as the old Grecian custom of removing the bride's coronet and putting her to bed. This particular form of ceremony was also found in Scotland, and continued to comparatively modern times. Young Scotch maidens formerly wore a snood, a sort of coronet, open at the top, called the virgin snood, and before being put to bed on the marriage night this snood was removed by the young women of the party. This custom is referred to in an ancient ballad.

> " They've ta'en the bride to the bridal bed,
> To loose her snood nae mind they had.
> ' I'll loose it,' quo John."

On the morning after some of the married women of the neighbourhood met in the young wife's house and put on her the *curtch* or close cap (*mutch*), a token of the marriage state. In my young days unmarried women went with the head uncovered; but after marriage, never

were seen without a cap. On the morning after marriage
the best man and maid breakfasted with the young
couple, after which they spent the day in the country,
or if they lived in the country, they went to town for
a change. Weddings were invariably celebrated on a
Friday,—the reason for this preference being, as is supposed, that Friday was the day dedicated by the Norse-
men to the goddess, Friga, the bestower of joy and happiness. The wedding day being Friday, the walking-
day was a Saturday; and on Sunday the young couple,
with their best man and best maid, attended church in the
forenoon, and took a walk in the afternoon, then spent
the evening in the house of one of their parents, the
meeting there being closed by family worship, and a
pious advice to the young couple to practise this in their
own house.

If the bride had been courted by other sweethearts
than he who was now her husband, there was a fear that
those discarded suitors might entertain unkindly feelings
towards her, and that their evil wishes might supernaturally influence her, and affect her first-born. This evil
result was sought to be averted by the bride wearing a
sixpence in her left shoe till she was *kirked;* but should
the bride have made a vow to any other, and broken it,
this wearing of the sixpence did not prevent the evil consequences from falling upon her first-born. Many instances were currently quoted among the people of first-
born children, under such circumstances, having been
born of such unnatural shapes and natures that, with the
sanction of the minister and the relations, the monster
birth was put to death. Captain Burt, in his letters from
the Highlands, written early in the eighteenth century,

says that "soon after the wedding day the newly-married wife sets herself about spinning her winding sheet, and a husband that shall sell or pawn it is esteemed among all men one of the most profligate." And Dr. Jamieson says—"When a woman of the lower class in Scotland, however poor, or whether married or single, commences housekeeping, her *first care*, after what is absolutely necessary for the time, is to provide *death linen* for herself and those who look to her for that office, and *her next* to earn, save, and *lay up (not put out to interest)* such money as may decently serve for funeral expenses. And many keep secret these honorable deposits and salutary *mementoes* for two or threescore years."

This practice was continued within my recollection. The first care of the young married wife was still, in my young days, to spin and get woven sufficient linen to make for herself and her husband their *dead claes*. I can well remember the time when, in my father's house, these things were spread out to air before the fire. This was done periodically, and these were days when mirth was banished from the household, and everything was done in a solemn mood. The day was kept as a Sabbath. The reader will not fail to observe in some of these modern customs and beliefs modified survivals of the old Roman practices and superstitious beliefs.

CHAPTER IV.

DEATH.

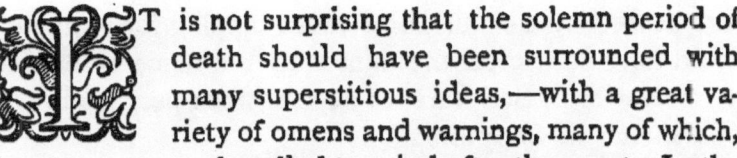T is not surprising that the solemn period of
death should have been surrounded with
many superstitious ideas,—with a great variety of omens and warnings, many of which,
however, were only called to mind after the event. In the
country, when any person was taken unwell, it was very
soon known over the whole neighbourhood, and all sorts
of remedies were recommended. Generally a doctor was
not sent for until the patient was considered in a dangerous state, and then began the search for omens or
warnings. If the patient recovered, these premonitions
were forgotten, but if death ensued, then everything was
remembered and rendered significant. Was a dog heard
to howl and moan during the night, with his head in the
direction of the house where the patient lay ; was there
heard in the silent watches of the night in the room
occupied by the sick person, a tick, ticking as of a watch
about the bed or furniture, these were sure signs of
approaching death, and adult patients hearing these
omens, often made sure that their end was near. Many
pious people also improved the circumstance, pointing
out that these omens were evidence of God's great mercy,
inasmuch as He vouchsafed to give a timely warning in
order that the dying persons might prepare for death,

and make their peace with the great Judge. To have hinted, under such circumstances, that the ticking sounds were caused by a small wood moth tapping for its mate, would have subjected the hinter to the name of infidel or unbeliever in Scripture, as superstitious people always took shelter in Scripture.

Persons hearing a tingling sound in their ears, called the *deid bells*, expected news of the death of a friend or neighbour. A knock heard at the door of the patient's room, and on opening no person being found, was a sure warning of approaching death. If the same thing occurred where there was no patient, it was a sign that some relation at a distance had died. I was sitting once in the house of a newly married couple, when a loud knock was heard upon the floor under a chair, as if some one had struck the floor with a flat piece of wood. The young wife removed the chair, and seeing nothing, remarked with some alarm, " It is hasty news of a death." Next day she received word of the death of two of her brothers, soldiers in India, the deaths having occurred nearly a year before. There was no doubt in the mind of the young wife that the knock was a supernatural warning. The natural explanation probably was that the sound came from the chair, which being new, was liable to shrink at the joints for some time, and thus cause the sound heard. This cracking sound is quite common with new furniture.

If, again, some one were to catch a glimpse of a person whom they knew passing the door or window, and on looking outside were to find no such person there, this was a sign of the approaching death of the person seen. There were many instances quoted of the accuracy of

this omen, instances generally of persons who, in good
health at the time of their illusionary presence, died
shortly after. Another form of this superstition was connected with those who were known to be seriously ill.
Should the observer see what he felt convinced was the
unwell person, say, walking along the street, and on
looking round as the presence passed, see no person, this
was a token of the death of the person whose spectre
was seen. I knew of a person who, on going home from
his work one evening, came suddenly upon an old man
whom he knew to be bed-ridden, dressed as was formerly
his wont, with knee breeches, blue coat, and red nightcap.
Although he knew that the old man had for some time
been confined to bed, so distinct was the illusion that he
bid him "good night" in passing, but receiving no reply,
looked behind and saw no one. Seized with fright, he
ran home and told what he had seen. On the following
morning it was known through the village that the old
man was dead. And his death had taken place at the
time when the young man had seen him on the previous
evening. This was considered a remarkably clear instance of a person's wraith or spirit being seen at the time
of death. However, the seeing of a person's wraith was
not always an omen of death. There were certain rules
observed in relation to wraiths, by which their meaning
could be ascertained, but these rules differed in different
localities. In my native village a wraith seen during
morning, or before twelve noon, betokened that the person whose wraith was seen would be fortunate in life, or
if unwell at the time, would recover ; but when the wraith
was seen in the afternoon or evening, this betokened evil
or approaching death, and the time within which death

would occur was considered to be within a year. This belief in wraiths goes back to a very early period of man's history. The ancient Persians and Jews believed that every person had a spirit or guardian angel attending him, and although generally invisible, it had the power of becoming visible, and separating itself for a time from the person it attended, and of appearing to other persons in the guise of the individual from whom it emanated. An excellent example of this superstitious belief is recorded in the Acts of the Apostles. When Peter, who was believed to be in prison, knocked at the "door of the gate" of the house where the disciples were met, the young woman who went to open the door, on recognising Peter's voice, was overjoyed, and, instead of opening, ran into the house, and told the disciples Peter was at the door. Then they said " It is his angel " (wraith). Thus the whole company expressed their belief in attending angels. The belief in wraiths was prevalent throughout all Scotland. It is beautifully introduced in the song of "Auld Robin Gray." When the young wife narrates her meeting with her old sweetheart, she says, " I thought it was his wraith, I could not think it he," and the belief survives in some parts of the country to the present day.

If a dying person struggled hard and long, it was believed that the spirit was kept from departing by some magic spell. It was therefore customary, under these circumstances, for the attendants to open every lock in the house, that the spell might be broken, and the spirit let loose. J. Train refers to this superstition in his *Mountain Muse*, published 1814 :—

" The chest unlocks to ward the power,
    Of spells in Mungo's evil hour."

After death there came a new class of superstitious
fears and practices. The clock was stopped, the looking-
glass was covered with a cloth, and all domestic animals
were removed from the house until after the funeral.
These things were done, however, by many from old custom, and without their knowing the reason why such
things were done. Originally the reason for the exclu-
sion of dogs and cats arose from the belief that, if either
of these animals should chance to leap over the corpse,
and be afterwards permitted to live, the devil would gain
power over the dead person.

When the corpse was laid out, a plate of salt was placed
upon the breast, ostensibly to prevent the body swelling.
Many did so in this belief, but its original purpose was to
act as a charm against the devil to prevent him from dis-
turbing the body. In some localities the plate of salt
was supplemented with another filled with earth. A
symbolical meaning was given for this ; that the earth
represented the corporeal body, the earthly house,—the
salt the heavenly state of the soul. But there was an
older superstition which gave another explanation for the
plate of salt on the breast. There were persons calling
themselves "*sin eaters*," who, when a person died, were
sent for to come and eat the sins of the deceased. When
they came, their *modus operandi* was to place a plate of
salt and a plate of bread on the breast of the corpse, and
repeat a series of incantations, after which they ate the
contents of the plates, and so relieved the dead person
of such sins as would have kept him hovering around
his relations, haunting them with his imperfectly purified

spirit, to their great annoyance, and without satisfaction to himself. This form of superstition has evidently a close relation to such forms of ancestor-worship as we know were practised by the ancients, and to which reference has already been made.

Until the funeral, it was the practice for some of the relations or friends to sit up all night, and watch the corpse. In my young days this duty was generally undertaken by youths, male and female friends, who volunteered their services; but these watchings were not accompanied by the unseemly revelries which were common in Scotland in earlier times, or as are still practised in Ireland. The company sitting up with the corpse generally numbered from two to six, although I have myself been one of ten. They went to the house about ten in the evening, and before the relations went to bed each received a glass of spirits; about midnight there was a refreshment of tea or ale and bread, and the same in the morning, when the relations of the deceased relieved the watchers. Although during these night sittings nothing unbefitting the solemnity of the occasion was done, the circumstances of the meeting gave opportunity for love-making. The first portion of the night was generally passed in reading,—some one reading aloud for the benefit of the company, afterwards they got to story-telling, the stories being generally of a ghostly description, producing such a weird feeling, that most of the company durst hardly look behind them for terror, and would start at the slightest noise. I have seen some so affected by this fear that they would not venture to the door alone if the morning was dark. These watchings of the dead were no doubt efficacious in perpetuating superstitious ideas.

The reasons given for watching the corpse differed in different localities. The practice is still observed, I believe, in some places; but probably now it is more the result of habit—a custom followed without any basis of definite belief, and merely as a mark of respect for the dead; but in former times, and within this century, it was firmly held that if the corpse were not watched, the devil would carry off the body, and many stories were current of such an awful result having happened. One such story was told me by a person who had received the story from a person who was present at the wake where the occurrence happened. I thus got it at second hand. The story ran as follows :—The corpse was laid out in a room, and the watchers had retired to another apartment to partake of refreshments, having shut the door of the room where the corpse lay. While they were eating there was heard a great noise, as of a struggle between two persons, proceeding from the room where the corpse lay. None of the party would venture into the room, and in this emergency they sent for the minister, who came, and, with the open ·Bible in his hand, entered the room and shut the door. The noise then ceased, and in about ten minutes he came out, lifted the tongs from the fireplace, and again re-entered the room. When he came out again, he brought out with the tongs a glove, which was seen to be bloody, and this he put into the fire. He refused, however, to tell either what he had seen or heard; but on the watchers returning to their post, the corpse lay as formerly, and as quiet and unruffled as if nothing had taken place, whereat they were all surprised.

From the death till the funeral it was customary for neighbours to call and see the corpse, and should any one see it and not touch it, that person would be haunted for several nights with fearful dreams. I have seen young children and even infants made to touch the face of the corpse, notwithstanding their terror and screams. If a child who had seen the corpse, but had not been compelled to touch it, had shortly afterwards awakened from a sleep crying, it would have been considered that its crying was caused by its having seen the ghost of the dead person.

If, when the funeral left the house, the company should go in a scattered, straggling manner, this was an omen that before long another funeral would leave the same house. If the company walked away quickly, it was also a bad omen. It was believed that the spirit of the last person buried in any graveyard had to keep watch lest any suicide or unbaptized child should be buried in the consecrated ground, so that, when two burials took place on the same day, there was a striving to be first at the churchyard. In some parts of the Highlands this superstition led to many unseemly scenes when funerals occurred on the same day.

Those attending the funeral who were not near neighbours or relations were given a quantity of bread and cakes to take home with them, but relations and near neighbours returned to the house, where their wives were collected, and were liberally treated to both meat and drink. This was termed the *dredgy* or *dirgy*, and to be present at this was considered a mark of respect to the departed. This custom may be the remnant of an ancient practice—in some sort a superstition—which existed in Greece, where the friends of the deceased, after the funeral, held a banquet, the fragments of which were afterwards carried to the tomb. Upon the death of a wealthy person, when the funeral had left the house, sums of money were divided among the poor. In Catholic times this was done that the poor might pray for the soul of the deceased. In the Danish *Niebellungen* song it is stated that, at the burial of the hero Seigfried, his wife caused upwards of thirty thousand merks of gold to be distributed among the poor for the welfare and repose of his soul. This custom became in this country and century in Protestant times an occasion for the gathering of beggars and sorners from all parts. At the funeral of George Oswald of Scotstoun, three miles from Glasgow, there were gathered several hundreds, who were each supplied with a silver coin and a drink of beer, and many were the blessings wished. A similar gathering occurred at the funeral of old Mr. Bogle of Gilmourhill, near Glasgow; but when announcement was made that nothing was to be given, there rose a fearful howl of execration and cursing both of dead and living from the mendacious crowd. The village of Partick in both these cases was placed under a species of black-mail for several days by beggars, who would hardly take any denial, and in many instances appropriated what was not their own. I am not aware that this custom is retained in any part of the country now.

As the funerals fifty years ago were mostly walking funerals, the coffin being carried between two spokes, the sort of weather during the funeral had its omens, for in these days the weather was believed to be greatly under the control of the devil, or rather it was considered that he was permitted to tamper with the weather. If the day was fine, this was naturally a good omen for the soul's welfare. I remember that the funeral of the only daughter of a worthy couple happened on a wet day, but just as the funeral was leaving the house the sun broke through and the day cleared, whereupon the mother, with evident delight, as she stood at the door, thanked God that Mary was getting a good blink. Stormy weather was a bad omen, being regarded as due to Satan's influence. Burns refers to this belief in his "Tam o' Shanter." When referring to the storm, he says :—

> " Even a bairn might understand
> The deil had business on his hand."

The following old rhyme mentions the most propitious sort of weather for the christening, marriage, and funeral :—

> " West wind to the bairn when gaun for its name,
> Gentle rain to the corpse carried to its lang hame,
> A bonny blue sky to welcome the bride,
> As she gangs to the kirk, wi' the sun on her side."

The wake in the Highlands during last century was a very common affair. Captain Burt, in his letters from Scotland, 1723, says that when a person dies the neighbours gather in the evening in the house where the dead lies, with bagpipe, and spend the evening in dancing— the nearest relative to the corpse leading off the dance. Whisky and other refreshments are provided, and this is continued every night until the funeral.

Pennant, in his tour through the Highlands, 1772, says that, at a death, the friends of the deceased meet with bagpipe or fiddle, when the nearest of kin leads off a melancholy ball, dancing and wailing at the same time, which continue till daybreak, and is continued nightly till the interment. This custom is to frighten off or protect the corpse from the attack of wild beasts, and evil spirits from carrying it away.

Another custom of olden times, and which was continued till the beginning of this century, was that of announcing the death of any person by sending a person with a bell—known as the "deid bell"—through the town or neighbourhood. The same was done to invite to the funeral. In all probability, the custom of ringing the bell had its origin in the church custom, being a call to offer prayers for the soul of the departed. Bell-ringing was also considered a means of keeping away evil spirits. Joseph Train, writing in 1814, refers to another practice common in some parts of Scotland. Whenever the corpse is taken from the house, the bed on which the deceased lay is taken from the house, and all the straw or heather of which it was composed is taken out and burned in a place where no beast can get at it, and in the morning the ashes are carefully examined, believing that the footprint of the next person of the family who will die will be seen. This practice of burning the contents of the bed is commendable for sanitary purposes.

CHAPTER V.

THAT the devil gave to certain persons super-natural power, which they might exercise at their pleasure, was a belief prevalent throughout all Scotland during the six-teenth and seventeenth centuries. But at the same time this compacting with the devil was reprobated, nay more, was a capital offence, both in civil and ecclesiastical law, and during these two centuries thousands of persons were convicted and executed for this crime. But during the latter part of the seventeenth century the civil courts re-fused to convict upon the usual evidence, to the great alarm and displeasure of the ecclesiastical authorities, who considered this refusal a great national sin—a direct violation of the law of God, which said—"Thou shalt not suffer a witch to live." To arrest the punishment which this direct violation of God's written law was sup-posed to incur, prayers were offered, and fasts were ap-pointed.

As samples of the kind of evidence on which reputed witches were convicted and executed, I extract the fol-lowing from the Records of Lanark Presbytery, 1650 : —"Likewise he reported that the Commissioners and "brethren did find these poynts delated against Janet "M'Birnie, one of the suspected women, to wit :

" 1st. That on a time the said Janet M'Birnie follow-
" ed Wm. Brown, sclater, to Robert Williamson's house
" in Water Meetings, to crave somewhat, and fell in evil
" words. After which time, and within four and twenty
" hours, he fell off ane house and brake his neck."

" 2nd. After some outcast between Bessie Achison's
" house and Janet M'Birnie's house, the said Janet
" M'Birnie prayed that there might be bloody beds and
" a light house, and after that the said Bessie Achison
" her daughter took sickness, and the lassie said there is
" fyre in my bed, and died. And the said Bessie
" Achison her gudeman dwyned.

" 3rd. It was alleged that the said Janet M'Birnie was
" the cause of the dispute between Newton and his wife,
" and that she and others were the death of William
" Geddese. And also that they fand against Marian
" Laidlaw, another suspected, these particulars : that the
" said Marian and Jean Blacklaw differed in words for
" the said Marian's hay ; and after that the said Jean
" her kye died."

They were remitted for trial. In these same Records
there is in 1697 the following entry :—" Upon the recom-
" mendation of the Synod, the Presbytery appoynts a
" Fast to be keeped upon the 28th instant, in regard to
" the great prevalence of witchcraft which abounds at
" several places at this time within the bounds of the
" Synod."

At this time the laws against witchcraft had become
practically a dead letter, but it was not till 1735 that
they were repealed. Still, the abolition of the legal
penalty did not kill the popular belief in the power and
reality of witchcraft ; and even now, at this present day,

we find proof every now and again in newspaper reports that this belief still lingers among certain classes. Within these fifty years, in a village a little to the west of Glasgow, lived an old woman, who was not poor, but had a very irritable temper, and was unsocial in her habits. A little boy having called her names and otherwise annoyed her, she scolded him, and, in the heat of her rage, prophesied that before a twelvemonth elapsed the devil would get his own. A few months after this the boy sickened and died, and the villagers had no hesitation in ascribing the cause of death to this old woman. Again, a farmer in the neighbourhood had bought a horse, and in the evening a servant was leading it to the water to drink, when this same old woman, who was sitting near at hand, remarked upon the beauty of the horse, and asked for a few hairs from the tail, which the servant with some roughness refused. When the stable was entered next morning the horse was found dead. On the above circumstance of the old woman's request being related to the farmer, he regretted the servant's refusal of the hairs, and said that, if the same woman had asked him, he would have given every hair in the tail rather than offend her, showing thereby his undoubted belief in the woman's power. Fortunately for her, she lived in a storeyed building—in local vernacular, a *land*—or in all probability her house would have been set on fire in order to burn her. At the same time, while she was hated and dreaded, everybody for their own safety paid her the most marked respect. Had she lived a century earlier, such evidence would have brought her to the stake. In 1666, before the Lanark Presbytery, a woman was tried for bewitching cattle :—

" The said William Smith said that she was the death
" of twa meires, and Elizabeth Johnstone, his wife, re-
" ported that she saw her sitting on their black meire's
" tether, and that she ran over the dyke in the likeness
" of a hare."

This belief in the ability of witches to convert themselves into the appearance of animals at pleasure was
prevalent even during this century.   In 1828, or there-
about, there died an old woman, who when alive had
gone about with a crutch, and it was reported of her,
and generally believed, that in her younger days she had
the power of witchcraft, and that one morning as she
was out about some of her unhallowed sports, disporting
herself in the shape of a hare, that a man who was out
with a gun saw, as he thought, in the moonlight, a hare,
and fired at it, breaking its leg ; but it took shelter
behind a stone, and when he went to get the hare, he
found instead a young woman sitting bandaging with a
handkerchief her leg, which was bleeding.   He knew her,
and upon her entreaty promised never to disclose her
secret, and ever after she went with a crutch.   I have
heard similar stories told of other women in other localities, showing the prevalence of this form of belief.   As
those who had dealings with the devil were believed to
have renounced their baptism or their allegiance to
Christ, they never went to church, and hated the Bible.
Therefore, all who did not follow the custom of believers
were not only considered infidels, but as having enlisted
in the devil's corps, and such people in small localities
were kept at an outside, and suspected, being regarded
as capable of any wickedness, and untrustworthy.   I
remember several persons, both men and women, against

intercourse with whom we were earnestly warned, and were instructed that it was not even safe to play with their children.

There were other supernatural powers thought to be possessed by certain persons, which differed from witchcraft in this, that they were not regarded as the result of a compact with the devil, but in some cases were thought to be rather a gift from God. For example, there was second-sight, a gift bestowed upon certain persons without any previous compact or solicitation. Sometimes the seer fell into a trance, in which state he saw visions; at other times the visions were seen without the trance condition. Should the seer see in a vision a certain person dressed in a shroud, this betokened that the death of that person would surely take place within a year. Should such a vision be seen in the morning, the person seen would die before that evening; should such a vision be seen in the afternoon, the person seen would die before next night; but if the vision were seen late in the evening, there was no particular time of death intimated, further than that it would take place within the year. Again, if the shroud did not cover the whole body, the fulfilment of the vision was at a great distance. If the vision were that of a man with a woman standing at his left hand, then that woman will be that man's wife, although they may both at the time of the vision be married to others. It was reported that one having second-sight saw in vision a young man with three women standing at his left side, and in course of time each became his wife in the order in which they were seen standing. These seers could often foretell coming visitors to a family months before they came, and even point out places where houses would be built years before the buildings were erected. The seer could not communicate the gift to any other person, not even to those of his own family, as he possessed it without any conscious act on his part ; but if any person were near him at the time he was having a vision, and he were consciously to touch the person with his left foot, the person touched would see that particular vision. I had a conversation with a woman who when young was in company with one who had the gift of second-sight. They went out together one Sabbath evening, and while sitting on the banks of the Kelvin the seer had a vision, and touched my informant with her left foot, and she also saw it. It rose from the water like the full moon, and was transparent ; and in it she saw a young man whom she did not know, and her own likeness standing at his left side. Before many weeks were passed, a new servant-man came to the farm where my informant was then serving, and whom she recognised as the person whose image she had seen in the vision, and in little more than a year after the two were married.

Deaf and dumb persons were considered to possess something like second-sight, by which they were enabled to foretell events which happen to certain persons. This is a very old belief. I extract the following from *Memorials of the Rev. R. Law :*—

" Anno 1676.—A daughter of the laird of Bardowie,
" in Badenoch parish, intending to go fra that to Hamil-
" ton to see her sister-in-law, there is at the same time a
" woman come into the house born deaf and dumb.
" She makes many signs to her not to go, and takes her
" down to the yaird and cutts at the root of a tree,

" making signs that it would fall and kill her.   That not
" being understood by her or any of them, she takes the
" journey—the dumb lass holding her to stay.   When the
" young gentlewoman is there at Hamilton, a few days
" after, her sister and she goes forth to walk in the park,
" and in their walking they both come under a tree.   In
" that very instant they come under it, they hear it shak-
" ing and coming down.   The sister-in-law flees to
" the right, and she herself flees to the left hand, that
" way that the tree fell, so it crushed her and wounded
" her sore, so that she dies in two or three days' sickness."

Until about 30 years ago, a deaf and dumb man was
in the habit of visiting my native village, who was believed
to possess wonderful gifts of foresight.   This *dummy*
carried with him a slate, a pencil, and a piece of chalk,
by use of which he gave his answers, and often he volunteered to give certain information concerning the future ;
he would often write down occurrences which he averred
would happen to parties in the village, or to pre-
sons then present.   He did not beg nor ask alms, but
only visited certain houses as a sort of friend, and information of his presence in the village was quickly conveyed
to the neighbours, so that he generally had a large gathering of women who were all friendly to him, and he was
never allowed to go away without reward.   When any
stranger was present he would point them out, and write
down the initials of their name, and sometimes their
names in full, without being asked.   He would also, at
times, write down the names of relatives of those present
who lived at a distance, and tell them when they would
receive letters from them, and whether these letters would
contain good or bad news.   He disclosed the whereabouts

K

of sailor lads and absent lovers, detected thefts, foretold
deaths and marriages, and the names of the parties
on both sides who were to be married. He wrote of a
young woman, a stranger in the village, but who was present on one of his visits, and was on the eve of being
married to a tradesman, that she would not be married
to him, but would marry one who would keep her count-
ing money; which came to pass. The tradesman and
she fell out, and afterwards she married a haberdasher,
and for a long time was in the shop as cashier. This
woman still lives, and firmly believes in the prophetic
gift of *dummy*. Another woman, a stranger also, asked
him some questions relative to herself; he shook his
head, and for a long time refused to answer, desiring her
not to insist. This made her the more anxious, and at
last he drew upon the slate the figure of a coffin. This
was all the length he would go. In less than twelve
months the woman was in her grave. During one of his
visits the husband of one of the women who attended
him was seriously ill, and the wife, a stout healthy woman,
was anxious to hear from *dummy* the result of her husband's illness. He wrote that the husband would recover,
and that she would die before him; and she did die not
long after. In short, this *dummy* was a regular prophet,
and his predictions were implicitly believed by all who
attended upon him. In his case there was no pretension
to visions, the form which he allowed his gift to assume
was that of intuition. Some few men in the village suspected the *dummy's* honesty, and thought that he heard
and assiduously and cunningly picked up knowledge of
the parties ; but such doubts were regarded as bordering
upon blasphemy by the believers in *dummy*. I was never

present at any of these gatherings, but my information is gathered from those who were present. Some months ago I was talking to an ordinarily intelligent person on this subject, and he gave it as his opinion that dumb persons had their loss of the faculties of hearing and speech recompensed to them in the gift of supernatural knowledge, and he related how a certain widow lady of his acquaintance had been informed of the death of her son. This son was abroad, and she had with her in the house a mute, who one day made signs to her that she would never see her son again, and a few weeks after she received word of his death.

There was another phase of supernatural power, different from witchcraft, and which the devil granted to certain parties : this was called the *Black Airt*. The possession of this power was mostly confined to Highlanders, and probably at this present day there are still those who believe in it. The effects produced by this power did not, however, differ much from those produced by witchcraft. A farmer in the north-west of Glasgow engaged a Highland lad as herd, and my informant also served with this farmer at the time. It was observed by the family that, after the lad came to them, everything went well with the farmer. During the winter, however, the *kye* became *yell*, and the family were consequently short of milk. The cows of a neighbouring farmer were at the same time giving plenty of milk. Under these circumstances, the Highland lad proposed to his mistress that he would bring milk from their neighbour's cows, which she understood to be by aid of the *black airt*, through the process known as *milking the tether*. The tether is the rope halter, and by going through the form of milking this, repeating certain incantations, the magic transference was supposed capable of being effected. This proposal to exercise the *black airt* becoming known among the servants, they were greatly alarmed, and showed their terror by all at once becoming very kind to the lad, and very watchful of what he did. He was known to have in his possession a pack of cards; and during family worship he displayed great restlessness, generally falling asleep before these services were concluded, and he was averse to reading the Bible. One night, for a few pence, he offered to tell the names of the sweethearts of the two servant-men, and they having agreed to the bargain, he shuffled the cards and said certain words which they did not understand, and then named two girls the lads were then courting. They refused to give him the promised reward, and he told them they would be glad to pay him before they slept. When the two men were going to their bed, which was over the stable, they were surprised to find two women draped in black closing up the stable door. As they stepped back, the women disappeared; but every time they tried to get in, the door was blocked up as before. The men then remembered what the lad had said to them, and going to where he slept, found him in bed, and gave him the promised reward. He then told them to go back, and they would not be further disturbed. Next morning, the servant-men told what had taken place, and refused to remain at the farm any longer with the lad; and the farmer had thus to part with him, but he and the servants gave him little gifts that they might part good friends. My informant believed himself above superstition, yet he related this as evidence of the truth of the *black airt*.

It is a very old belief that those who had made compacts with the devil could afflict those they disliked with certain diseases, and even cause their death, by making images in clay or wax of the persons they wished to injure, and then, by baptizing these images with mock ceremony, the persons represented were brought under their influence, so that whatever was then done to the image was felt by the living original. This superstition is referred to by Allan Ramsay in his *Gentle Shepherd :—*

> " Pictures oft she makes
> Of folk she hates, and gaur expire
> Wi' slow and racking pain before the fire.
> Stuck fu' o' preens, the devilish picture melt,
> The pain by folk they represent is felt."

This belief survived in great force in this century, and probably in country places is not yet extinct. Several persons have been named to me who suffered long from diseases the doctor could not understand, nor do anything to remove, and therefore these obscure diseases could only be ascribed to the devil-aided practices of malicious persons. In some cases, cures were said to have been effected through making friends of the supposed originators of the disease. The custom not yet extinct of burning persons in effigy is doubtless a survival of this old superstition.

A newly-married woman with whom I was acquainted took a sudden fit of mental derangement, and screamed and talked violently to herself. Her friends and neighbours concluded that she was under the spell of the evil one. The late Dr. Mitchell was sent for to pray for her, but when he began to pray she set up such hideous screams that he was obliged to stop. He advised her friends to call in medical aid.   But this conduct on the part of the woman made it all the more evident to her relations and neighbours that her affliction was the work of the devil, brought about through the agency of some evil-disposed person.   Several such persons were suspected, and sent for to visit the afflicted woman ; and, while they were in the house, a relation of the sufferer's secretly cut out a small portion of the visitor's dress and threw it into the fire, by which means it was believed that the influence of the *ill ée* would be destroyed.   At all events, the woman suddenly got well again, and as a consequence the superstitious belief of those who were in the secret was strengthened.

CHAPTER VI.

CHARMS AND COUNTER CHARMS.

URING these times when such superstitious beliefs were almost universally accepted—when the sources from which evils might be expected to spring were about as numerous as the unchecked fancies of men could make them —we must naturally conceive that the people who believed such things must have lived in a continual state of fear. And in many instances this was really the case ; but the common result was not so, for fortunately the bane and antidote were generally found together, and the means for preventing or exorcising these devil-imposed evils were about as numerous as the evils themselves. I have already in a former chapter mentioned incidentally some of these charms and preventives, but as this incidental treatment cannot possibly cover the field, I shall here speak of them separately.

Tennant, in his *Tour through Scotland*, states that farmers placed boughs of the mountain ash in their cow-houses on the second day of May to protect their cows from evil influences. The rowan tree possessed a wonderful influence against all evil machinations of witchcraft. A staff made of this tree laid above the boothy or milk-house preserved the milk from witch influence. A churn-staff made of this wood secured the butter during the process of churning. So late as 1860 I have seen the rowan tree trained in the form of an arch over the byre door, and in another case over the gate of the farm-yard, as a protection to the cows. It was also believed that a rowan tree growing in a field protected the cattle against being struck by lightning.

Mr. Train describes the action of a careful farmer's wife or dairymaid thus :—

> " Lest witches should obtain the power
> Of Hawkie's milk in evil hour,
> She winds a red thread round her horn,
> And milks thro' row'n tree night and morn ;
> Against the blink of evil eye
> She knows each andidote to ply."

The same author, writing in 1814, says :—" I am ac-quainted myself with an Anti-Burgher clergyman who actually procured from a person who pretended to such skill in these charms two small pieces of carved wood, to be kept in his father's cow-house as a security for the health of his cows." The belief in the potency of the rowan tree to ward off evil is no doubt a survival of ancient tree worship. Of this worship, the Rev. F. W. Farrar says :—" It may be traced from the interior of Africa, not only in Egypt and Arabia, but also onwards uninterruptedly into Palestine and Syria, Assyria, Persia, India, Thibet, Siam, the Philippine Islands, China, Japan, and Siberia ; also westward into Asia Minor, Greece, Italy, and other countries ; and in most of the countries here named it obtains at the present day, combined, as it has been, in other parts with various forms of idolatry." Were it our object, it could also be shown that tree worship has been combined with

Christianity. The rowan tree was held sacred by the Druids, and is often found among their stone monuments. There is a northern legend that the god of thunder (Thor), when wading the river Vimar, was in danger of being swept away by its current, but that, grasping a tree which grew on the bank, he got safely across. This tree was the mountain ash, which was ever after held sacred; and when these nations were converted to Christianity, they did not fall away from their belief in the sanctity of the rowan tree.

Not many years ago, I was told of a miraculous make of butter which was reported to have occurred in the west of Lanarkshire a short time before. One morning, a farmer's wife in that district and her maid-servant wrought at the kirn, but, do as they would, no butter would appear. In this dilemma, they sat down to consider about the cause, and then they recollected that a neighbouring woman had come into the kitchen, where the kirn was standing the previous evening, to borrow something, but was refused. The servant was at once despatched with the article in question, and half-a-dozen eggs as a gift, to the old woman, and instructed to make an apology for not having given the loan the evening before. The woman received the gift, and gratefully expressed her wish that the farmer and his wife would be blest both in their basket and their store. The effect, said my informant, was miraculous. Before the servant returned, the butter began to flow, and in such quantity as had never before been experienced.

Apropos of this superstition with reference to milk, the following incident occurred not many years back in the West Highlands. An old woman, who kept a few cows, was in sore distress of mind because some of her ill-disposed neighbours had cast an evil eye upon them, in consequence of which their milk in a very short time *blinked* (turned sour), and churn as she might, she could never obtain any butter. She had tried every remedy she knew of, or that had been recommended to her, but without any good effect. At length, in her extremity, she applied to the parish minister, and laid her case before him. He patiently listened to her complaint, and expressed great sympathy for her, and then very wisely said, " I'll tell you how I think you will succeed in driving away the evil eye. It seems to me that it has not been cast on your cows, but on your dishes. Gang hame and tak' a' your dishes down to the burn, and let them lie awhile in the running stream ; then rub them well and dry with a clean clout. Tak' them hame and fill each with boiling water. Pour it out and lay them aside to dry. The evil eye cannot withstand boiling water. Sca'd it out and ye'll get butter." The prescription was followed, and a few weeks after the woman called upon the minister and thanked him for the cure, remarking that she had never seen anything so wonderful.

Mr. Joseph Train, from whose notes we have already quoted, mentions a ceremony, not of a private but of a public nature, and embracing a large district of country, at the performance of which he was present. The object to be obtained was the prevention of a threatened outbreak of disease among the cattle. " In the summer of 1810," says Mr. Train, " while remaining at Balnaguard, a village of Perthshire, as I was walking along the banks of the Tay, I observed a crowd of people

convened on the hill above Pitna Cree ; and as I recollected having seen a multitude in the same place the
preceding day, my curiosity was roused, so that I resolved
to learn the reason of this meeting in such an unfre-
quented place. I was close beside them before any of
the company had observed me ascending the hill, their
attention being fixed upon two men in the centre. One
was turning a small stock, which was supported by two
stakes standing perpendicularly, with a cleft at the top,
in which the crown piece went round in the form a
carpenter holds a chisel on a grinding stone ; the other
was holding a small branch of fir on that which was
turning. Directly below it was a quantity of tow spread
on the ground. I observed that this work was taken
alternately by men and women. As I was turning
about in order to leave them, a man whom I had seen
before, laid his hand on my shoulder, and solicited me
to put my finger to the stick ; but I refused, merely to
see if my obstinacy would be resented ; and suddenly
a sigh arose from every breast, and anger kindled in
every eye. I saw, therefore, that immediate compliance
with the request was necessary to my safety.

" I was soon convinced that this was some mysterious
rite performed either to break or ward off the power of
witchcraft ; but, so intent were they on the prosecution
of their design, that I could obtain no satisfactory
information, until I met an old schoolmaster in the
neighbourhood, from whom I had obtained much in-
sight into the manners and customs of that district. He
informed me that there is a distemper occasioned by
want of water, which cattle are subject to, called in the
Gaelic language *shag dubh*, which in English signifies

'black haunch.' It is a very infectious disease, and, if not taken in time, would carry off most of the cattle in the country." The method taken by the High-landers to prevent its destructive ravages is thus : " All fires are extinguished between the two nearest rivers, and all the people within that boundary convene in a convenient place, where they erect a machine, as above described ; and, after they have commenced, they con-tinue night and day until they have forced fire by the friction of the two sticks. Every person must perform a portion of this labour, or touch the machine in order not to break the charm.

" During the continuance of the ceremony they appear melancholy and dejected, but when the fire, which they say is brought from heaven by an angel, blazes in the tow, they resume their wonted gaiety ; and while one part of the company is employed feeding the flame, the others drive all the cattle in the neighbourhood over it. When this ceremony is ended, they consider the cure complete ; after which they drink whiskey, and dance to the bagpipe or fiddle round the celestial fire till the last spark is extinguished."

Here, within our own day, is evidently an act of fire-worship : a direct worship of Baal by a Christian com-munity in the nineteenth century. There were other means of preventing disease spreading among cattle practised within this century. When murrain broke out in a herd, it was believed that, if the first one taken ill were buried alive, it would stop the spread of the disease, and that the other animals affected would then soon re-cover. Were a cow to cast her calf: if the calf were to be buried at the byre door, and a short prayer or a verse of

Scripture said over it, it would prevent the same misfortune from happening with the rest of the herd. If a sheep dropped a dead lamb, the proper precaution to take was to place the lamb upon a rowan tree, and this would prevent the whole flock from a repetition of the mishap.

It was an old superstition that the body of a murdered person would bleed on the presence or touch of the murderer. We find this belief mentioned as far back as the eleventh century. In an old ballad of that period occurs the following passage :—

> " A marvel high and strange is seen full many a time—
> When to the murdered body nigh the man that did the crime,
> Afresh the wounds will bleed. The marvel now was found—
> That Hagan felled the champion with treason to the ground."

Several centuries after this, we find it mentioned in another ballad, entitled " Young Huntin " :—

> " O white were his wounds washen,
>   As white as a linen clout,
> But when Lady Maisry she cam' near,
>   His wounds they gushed out."

The reason for this marvel was ascribed by the Rev. Mr. Wodrow, to the wonderful providence of God, who had said, " thou shalt not suffer a murderer to live," and had, in order that the command might be justly carried out, provided the means whereby murderers might be readily detected. This superstition certainly survived within this century, and I have heard many instances adduced to prove the truth of bleeding taking place on the introduction of the murderer.

Another curious form of belief was prevalent among

some persons, that the body of a suicide would not decay until the time arrived when, in the ordinary course of nature, he would have died. This was founded upon another belief, that there is a day of death appointed for every man, which no one can pass; but as man is possessed of a free will, he may, by his own wicked determination, shorten the union of his soul and body, but that there his power ends : he cannot in reality kill either soul or body, for were he to possess this power, he would possess the power to alter the decrees of God, which is a power impossible for man to possess. This was a mad, not deep, sort of metaphysics; but there was sufficient method in its madness to cause it to gain the suffrages of a large number of people. It was affirmed that those who had examined into the matter had found that the bodies of suicides were mysteriously preserved from decomposition until the day arrived on which they would naturally—that is, according to God's decree—have died. About the year 1834, I was taking a walk along the banks of the canal north of Glasgow, and sat down beside a group of well-dressed men, who were conversing on general topics, and amongst other things touched on the matter of suicides—proximity to the canal probably suggested the subject. One of the group pointed out a quiet spot where he affirmed that *Bob Dragon*, an old Glasgow celebrity, had been buried. Bob, he said, had committed suicide ; but his relations being aware that, in consequence of this act, his property, according to law, became forfeited to the Crown, had him buried secretly in this out-of-the-way spot, and obtained another corpse, which they put into the coffin in his house. But, several years after, some persons who were digging at this quiet spot on the canal bank discovered the real body of Bob—the throat being cut—and the corpse as fresh as the day on which the act was committed. Bob's relations, on hearing of this discovery, gave the finders a handsome gift to rebury the body and keep the matter secret. Within the last ten years I have heard the same affirmation made respecting persons who have drowned themselves.

Persons whose *yea* is unvaryingly *yea*, and whose *nay* is unvaryingly *nay*, generally resort to no form of oath or imprecation to gain credence to their statements, for their truthfulness is seldom called in question—at least, where they are well known. But with those who are lax in their statements—who tell the truth or tell lies just as for the moment the one or the other appears to suit them best—the case is different. When they speak something strange or important, they find their veracity questioned, and require to place themselves in circumstances where it may be thought they are under compulsion, for their own welfare, to speak the truth. Commonly, they ask Providence to injure them in some way if in the present instance they have said the thing which is not true. Well, it was believed in the days of which I write, and within my own day, that Providence did interfere in this way, and many stories were current in confirmation of this belief. One such will suffice as an illustration. A married woman, *enciente* for the first time, having had words with her husband about something she denied having either said or done, wished that, if her statement were untrue, she might never give birth to the child. She was taken at her word, for she lived many years in delicate health, but the child was

never born. The villagers who remembered her said
that at times she *swelled* as if she was about to be confined, and at other times was as *jimp* as a young girl.

Akin to belief in the potency of such wishes as were
uttered as tests of truthfulness was doubtless the generally
accredited, though of course seldom witnessed, form of
compact with the devil. When a person agreed to serve
the devil, his Satanic Majesty caused the mortals who
sought his service and favour to place one hand under
their thigh and the other over their head, and wish
that the devil would take all that lay between their
hands if they were unfaithful to their vow. The form of
oath by expression of a wish was common to both Jews
and Gentiles.

There was another kind of wish which was believed to
obtain fulfilment during life, that was the expressed wish
of the innocent against those who had wronged them.
The belief in the fulfilment of such wishes was grounded
on the theological supposition that God in his justice
would in time punish the wrong-doer. I remember a
rather pertinent example of this : a proof they would have
said in former days—a coincidence we would say in
these days. A simple-minded — *half-witted* — young
woman was taken advantage of by a young man resident
in the neighbourhood, to the public scandal of the village. He denied the paternity of the baby, and made
oath to that effect before the kirk-session. As he did so,
the girl, looking at him, wished that the hand he held up
might lose its cunning, as evidence of God's judgment
upon the false swearer. In less than a year from that
time a disease came into his right hand, and he was
never afterwards able to use it. Not many years ago, I

saw the same man going through the village selling tea, and, as he passed along the street, many of the older inhabitants remarked how wonderfully *Poor Meg's* wish had been fulfilled.

Employment of certain charms to influence for good or evil prevailed in this century to a great extent. Some of these it is difficult to trace to their origin. About forty years ago, a certain married couple lived unhappily together. The wife did all she could to make her husband comfortable, but still he abused her without cause. At length, after suffering much, she applied to a woman who professed to have power over the affections, and for this purpose prepared love philters. The woman gave her a charm, which was to be sewn between the lining and cloth of her husband's vest without his knowledge. She carried these instructions out, and with extraordinarily successful results, for, while the husband wore this vest, he never gave her so much as an angry word.

One Walter Donaldson was in the habit of beating his wife, and making her life bitter. She made application to Isabell Straguhan, who possesses magic influences, who took pieces of paper and sewed them thick with thread of divers colours, and put them in the barn among the corn. From that time forth the said Walter never lifted hand against his wife, nor did once find fault with her whatsoever she did, and was entirely subdued to her love.

The following was related to me as a fact, by a person who said that he tried it :—There is a certain crooked bone in a frog, which, when cleaned and dried over a fire on St. John's eve, and then ground fine and given in food to any person, will win the affections of the receiver to the giver, and in young persons will produce a desire for each other's society, culminating eventually in marriage; also, when a married couple do not agree well together, it will reconcile them, and bring about a mutual affection.

At the commencement of this century, belief in the influence of the mandrake plant over the affections still existed in this country. Belief in this plant is as old as history. Leah, the neglected wife of Jacob, doubtless intended to influence her husband by the use of it, whilst Rachel procured the plant for a different purpose, but for both purposes it was considered efficatious, and in both cases, the narrative shows, successful. By both eastern and western nations this plant was credited with wonderful powers, even to the extent of working miracles. In this country it was believed to be watched by Satan, but if the plant were pulled during certain holy seasons, or by holy persons, Satan would not only be robbed with impunity, but he would become the servant of the person who pulled the plant, and do for him whatever he desired; but woe to the unholy person who attempted to pull the plant, especially at a non-sacred time; he drops down dead, and Satan possesses his soul.

It was a prevalent belief that the seventh son in a family had the gift of curing diseases, and that he was by nature a doctor who could effect cures by the touch of his hand. It was reported that such a man resided in Iona, who had effected cures by rubbing the diseased part with his hand on two Thursdays and two Sundays successively, doing so in the name of the Father, the Son, and the Holy Ghost. It was requisite to the cure that no fee should be taken by such endowed persons.   In the West of Scotland the formula of cure was different in different localities; in some parts a mere touch was all that was necessary, in others, and this was the more general method, some medicine was given to assist the cure.

Written charms were also believed in as capable of effecting cures, or, at least, of preventing people from taking diseases.   I have known people who wore written charms, sewed into the necks of their coats, if men, and into the headbands of petticoats if women.   These talismans, in many cases, I have little doubt, did real good in this way, that they supplied their wearers with a courage which sufficed to brace up their nervous system —which drove out fear, in fact,—a very important condition for health, as physicians well know.   These talismans were so generally and thoroughly believed in, and so numerous and apparently well-attested were the evidences of their beneficial effects, that in years not long past, medical men believed in their efficacy, and promulgated various theories to account for it.

It was also an accepted belief that diseases could be transferred to animals, and even to vegetables.   Cures held to be so effected were, according to one medical theory, cures by "sympathy."   A few instances, culled from a work published during the latter half of the seventeenth   century   (1663),   entitled   *The Usefulness of Experimental Philosophy*,   will   illustrate this   theory :— A medical man had been very ill of an obstinate *marasmar* (?) which so consumed him that he became quite a skeleton, notwithstanding every remedy which he had tried.   At length he tried a sympathetic remedy : he took an egg, and having boiled it hard in his own urine, he then with a bodkin perforated the shell in different parts, and then buried it in an ant-hill. As the ants wasted the egg he found his strength increase, and he soon was completely cured. A daughter of a French officer was so tormented by a *paronychia* (?) for four days together, that the pain kept her from sleeping; by the order of a medical man she put her finger into a cat's ear, and within two hours was delivered from her pain. And a councillor's wife was cured of a *panaritium* (?) which had vexed her for four days by the same means. In both cases the cat had received the pain in its ear and required to be held. The gout is cured by sympathy: by the patient sleeping with puppies, they take the disease, and the person recovers. A boy ill with the king's evil could not be cured, his father's dog took to licking the sores, the dog took the sores, and the boy was completely cured. A gentleman having a severe pain in the arm was cured by beating red coral with oak leaves, and applying it to the part affected till suppuration : a hole was then made in the root of an oak towards the east, and the mixture put into it and the hole plugged up with a peg of the same tree, and from that time the pain did altogether cease ; and when afterwards the mixture was removed from the tree, immediately the torments returned worse than before. Sir Francis Bacon records a cure of warts : he took a piece of lard with the skin on it, and after rubbing the warts with it the the lard was exposed out of a southern window to putrify, and the warts wore away as it putrified. Harvey tried to remove tumours and excrescences by putting the hand of a dead person that had died of a lingering disease upon them till the part felt cold. In general the application was effective.

This idea of cure by sympathy retained its hold on the people till this century, and is not yet entirely gone.

There was another theory, which we may call the magnetic theory. The philosophy of this theory contended that "The body when diseased resembled a gun ; when loaded, it contains powder and ball, which, by the mere touch of a little spring, sets the whole machinery of the gun in motion, whereby the ball is expelled. So also the mere touch or outward contact of certain bodies or substances has power, like a magnet, to set in action the machinery of nature by which the disease is dispelled—sometimes slowly, but often suddenly like the bullet from the gun. Helmont had a little stone, which, by plunging in oil of almonds, imbued the oil with such sanative power that it cured almost any disease. It was sometimes applied inwardly, sometimes outwardly. A gentleman who had an unweildy groom procured for him a small fragment of this stone, and, by licking it with the tip of his tongue every morning, in three weeks he was reduced in bulk round the waist by a span without affecting his general health. A gentleman in France who procured a small fragment of this stone cured several persons of inveterate diseases by letting them lick it. The stone *Lapis Nephriticus* bound upon the pulse of the wrist of the left hand prevents stone, hysterics, and stops the flux of blood in any part. A compound metal called *electrum*, which is a mixture of all metals made under certain constellations and shaped into rings and worn, prevents cramps and palsy, apoplexy, epilepsy, and se-

vere pains; and in the case of a person in a fit of the
falling sickness, a ring of this metal put on the ring finger is an immediate cure.   A little yarrow and mistletoe put into a bag and worn upon the stomach, prevents ague and chilblains.   A powder made of the
common mistletoe, given in doses of three grains at the
full of the moon to persons troubled with epilepsy, prevents fits; and if given during a fit it will effect an
immediate and permanent cure.   A woman with rupture of the bladder was reported to have been cured
by wearing a little bag hung about her neck containing
the powder made from a toad burnt alive in a new pot.
The same prescription was also said to have cured a
man of stone in the bladder."

Such theories left ample room for the creation of all
sorts of cure charms, and when such ideas prevailed
among the educated in the medical profession, we need
not be surprised that they still survive among many un-
educated persons, although two centuries have gone since.
In 1714 one of the most eminent physicians in Europe, Boer-
haave, wrote of chemistry and medicine:—"Nor even in this
affair don't medicine receive some advantage; witness
the cups made of regulus of antimony, tempered with
other metals which communicate a medicinal quality to
wine put in them, and it is ten thousand pities the
famous *Von Helmont* should have been so unkind to his
poor fellow creatures in distress as to conceal from us
the art of making a particular metal which he tells
us, made into rings, and worn only while one might say
the Lord's Prayer, would remove the most exquisite hæ-
morrhoidal pains, both internal and external, quiet the
most violent hysteric disorders, and give ease in the sc-

verest spasms of the muscles. 'Tis right, therefore, to prosecute enquiries of this nature, for there is very frequently some hidden virtues in these compositions, and we may make a vast number of experiments of this kind without any danger or inconvenience."

As it illustrates the theories just mentioned, we notice here the influence attributed to the wonderful Lee Penny. This famous charm is a stone set in gold. It is said to have been brought home by Lochart of Lee, who accompanied the Earl of Douglas in carrying Robert the Bruce's heart to the Holy Land. It is called Lee Penny, and was credited with the virtue of imparting to water into which it was dipped curative properties, specially influential to the curing of cattle when diseased, or preventing them taking disease. Many people from various parts of Scotland whose cattle were affected have made application within these few years for water in which this stone has been dipped. It is believed that this stone cannot be lost. It is still in the possession of the family of Lochart.

Ague, it was believed, could be cured by putting a spider into a goose quill, sealing it up, and hanging it about the neck, so that it would be near the stomach. This disease might also be cured by swallowing pills made of a spider's web. One pill a morning for three successive mornings before breakfast.

There were numerous cures for hooping-cough of a superstitious character, practised extensively during the earlier years of this century, and some are still recommended. The following are a few of these. Pass the patient three times under the belly, and three times over the back of a donkey. Split a sapling or a branch of the ash tree, and hold the split open while the patient is passed three times through the opening. Find a man riding on a piebald horse, and ask him what should be given as a medicine, and whatever he prescribes will prove a certain cure. "I recollect, says Jamieson, "a friend of mine that rode a piebald horse, that he used to be pursued by people running after him bawling,—

> " Man wi' the piety horse,
> What's gude for the kink host?"

He said he always told them to give the bairn plenty of sugar candy. Put a piece of *red* flannel round the neck of a child, and it will ward off the hooping cough. The virtue lay not in the flannel, but in the red colour. Red was a colour symbolical of triumph and victory over all enemies. Find a hairy caterpillar, put it into a bag, and hang it round the neck of the child. This will prove a cure. Take some of the child's hair and put it between slices of bread and butter, and give it to a dog; if in eating it, the dog cough, the child will be cured, and the hooping cough transferred to the dog. A very common practice at the present day is to take the patient into a place where there is a tainted atmosphere, such as a byre or a stable, a gas work, or chemical work. I have seen the gas blown on the child's face, so that it might breath some of it, and be set a coughing. If during the process the child take a *kink*, it is a good sign. This idea must, I think, be of modern origin.

It was believed that if a present were given, especially if it were given to a sweetheart, and then asked back again, the giver would have a stye on the eye. Again, a stye on the eye was removable by rubbing it with a wedding ring. I suspect these two superstitions are portions of an ancient allegory, which, in time loosing their figurative meanings, came to be treated as literal facts.

Warts, especially when they are upon exposed parts of the body, are sometimes a source of annoyance to their possessors, and various and curious methods were taken for their removal. From their position on the body they also were regarded as prognostications of good or bad luck. To have warts on the right hand foreboded riches; a wart on the face indicated troubles of various kinds.

We have already noticed the cure recommended by the learned Sir Francis Bacon. The following are a few of the cures which were believed in within this century. Rub the wart with a piece of stolen bacon. Rub the wart with a black snail, and lay the snail upon a hedge or dyke. As the animal decays so will the wart. Wash the wart with sow's blood for three days in succession.

Upon the first sight of the new moon stand still and take a small portion of earth from under the right foot, make it into a paste, put it on the wart and wrap it round with a cloth, and thus let it remain till that moon is out. The moon's influence and the fasting spittle are very old superstitions.

The moon or Ashtoreth, the consort of Baal, was the great female deity of the ancients, and so an appeal to the moon for the purpose of removing interferences with beauty, such as skin excrescences, was quite appropriate. Moon worship was practised in this country in prehistoric times. Bailey, in his *Etymological Dictionary*, under article "Moon," says, "The moon was an ancient idol of England, and worshipped by the Britons in the form of a beautiful maid, having her head covered, with two ears standing out. The common people in some counties of England are accustomed at the prime of the moon to say '*It is a fine moon. God bless her.*'"

From a custom in Scotland (particularly in the Highlands) where the young women make courtesy to the new moon by getting upon a gate or style and sitting astride, they say—

> " All hail to the moon, all hail to thee,
> I prithee good moon declare to me
> This very night who my husband shall be."

Every one knows the popular adage about having money in the pocket when the new moon is first seen, and that if the coins be turned over at the time, money will not fail you during that moon. To see the new moon through glass, however, breaks the charm. It was a prevalent belief that if a person on catching the first glimpse of new moon, were to instantly stand still, kiss their hand three times to the moon, and bow to it, that they would find something of value before that moon was out. Such practices are evidently survivals of moon worship. How closely does this last practice agree with what Job says (chap. xxxi, 26),—"If I beheld the sun when it shined, or the moon walking in brightness, and my heart hath been secretly enticed, or my mouth hath kissed my hand : this also were an iniquity to be punished by the Judge: for I should have denied the God that is above."

The good influence of the fasting spittle in destroying the influence of an evil eye has been already referred to in the previous pages, but it was also esteemed a potent remedy in curing certain diseases. To moisten a wart for several days in succession with the fasting spittle removes it. I have often seen a nurse bathe the eyes of a baby in the morning Aith her fasting spittle, to cure or prevent sore eyes. I have heard the same cure recommended for roughness of the skin and other skin diseases. Maimonides states that the Jews were expressly forbidden by their traditions to put fasting-spittle upon the eyes on the Sabbath day, because to do so was to perform work, the great Sabbath crime in the eyes of the Pharisees which Christ committed when he moistened the clay with his spittle and anointed the eyes of the blind man therewith on the Sabbath day. To both Greeks and Romans the fasting spittle was a charm against fascination. Persius Flaccus says :—"A grandmother or a superstitious aunt has taken baby from his cradle, and is charming his forehead and his slavering lips against mischief by the joint action of her middle finger and her purifying spittle." Here we find that it is not the spittle alone, but the joint action of the spittle and the middle finger which works the influence. The middle finger was commonly, in the early years of this century, believed to possess a favourable influence on sores ; or, rather, it might be more correct to say that it possessed no damaging influence, while all the other fingers, in coming into contact with a sore, were held to have a tendency to defile, to poison, or canker the wound. I have heard it asserted that doctors know this, and never touch a sore but with the mid-finger.

There were other practices and notions appertaining to the spittle and spitting, some of which continue to this day. To spit for luck upon the first coin earned or gained by trading, before putting it into the pocket or purse, is a common practice. To spit in your hand before grasping the hand of a person with whom you are dealing, and whose offer you accept, is held to clinch the bargain, and make it binding on both sides. This is a very old custom. Captain Burt, in his letters, says that when in a bargain between two Highlanders, each of them wets the ball of his thumb with his mouth, and then they press their wet thumb balls together, it is esteemed a very binding bargain. Children in their games, which are often imitations of the practices of men, make use of the spittle. When playing at games of chance, such as *odds or evens*, *something or nothing*, etc., before the player ventures his guess he consults an augury, of a sort, by spitting on the back of his hand, and striking the spittle with his mid-finger, watching the direction in which the superfluous spittle flies, from him or to him, to right or left, and therefrom, by a rule of his own, he determines what shall be his guess. Again, boys often bind one another to a bargain or promise by a sort of oath, which is completed by spitting. It runs thus :

> " Chaps ye, chaps ye,
> Double, double daps ye,
> Fire aboon, fire below,
> Fire on every side o' ye."

After saying this, the boy spits over his head three times, and without this the oath is not considered binding ; but when properly done, and the promise not fulfilled, the defaulter is regarded as a liar, and is kept for a time at an outside by his companions.

When two boys made an arrangement (I am speaking of what was the custom fifty years back), either to meet together at a stated time or to do some certain thing, the arrangement was confirmed by each spitting on the ground.

When a number of boys or girls were trying to find out a puzzle or guess put to them, and which they failed to unravel or answer, and when they were searching for something which had been hidden from them, and which they could not discover, the usual method of acknowledging that they were outwitted was by spitting on the ground; in the language of the day, they would be requested to "spit and gie't o'er," that is, own that they were beaten. The propounder of the puzzle, or the party who had hidden the object, was then bound to disclose the matter.

When two boys quarrelled, and one wet the other boy's buttons with his spittle, this was a challenge to fight or be dubbed a coward.

Mahomet held that bad dreams were from the devil, and advised the dreamers to seek protection by addressing a short prayer to God, and then spitting three times over their left shoulder. He further counselled them to tell the dream to no one, and by following these instructions no harm, such as the dreams had foreshadowed, would befal them.

In the case of a person bitten by a dog, a few hairs taken from the dog's tail, and placed upon the wound either upon or under a poultice, was regarded as a protection from evil consequences, such as hydrophobia. I know of an instance in which this remedy was applied so lately as 1876. This practice is unmistakeably the origin of the toper's proverb when suffering from headache in the morning,

" Take a hair of the dog that bit you."

I will not enter into the subject of faith in the influence of relics. Such beliefs existed in Scotland in my young days, and it is almost unnecessary to say that belief in such things is older than history. In my youth there was also a belief in the virtue of precious stones, which added a value to them beyond their real value as ornaments. An investigation into this matter would tend to throw much light upon many ancient practices and beliefs, as each stone had its own symbolic meaning, and its own peculiar influence for imparting good and protecting from evil and from sickness, its fortunate possessor. Probably John's description of heaven with its windows of agate, its doors of pearls or carbuncles, its foundations of amethyst, with sapphires blue, and sardines clear and red, had relation to the popular beliefs of the time. I have seen at Mill More, Killin, stones which are reported to have been used by St. Fillan for curing all sorts of diseases ; and there are not a few persons at the present day who wear certain polished stones about their persons as a protective influence against certain diseases.

The ancient Jews had a superstitious idea respecting precious stones, which gave that strong desire for their possession, which is still characteristic of the race.

The Diamond was an antidote to Satanic temptation.

Ruby made the possessor brave.

Topaz preserved the bearer against being poisoned.

Amethyst preserved from drunkenness.

Emerald promoted piety.

Sardonyx dispelled unholy thoughts.

There is a legend that God gave to Abraham a precious stone which had the power of preserving him from all kinds of sickness.

When any person was troubled with a morbid hunger accompanied with pain in the stomach, it was believed that that affliction was caused by the sufferer having swallowed some animal, which continued to live in the stomach, and that when this was empty it knawed the stomach and produced the pain felt. Several strange instances illustrative of the truth of this theory were current in my native village. Let one case suffice. An old soldier having on some long march been induced through extreme thirst to drink from a ditch, had swallowed some animal. Years after he was taken ill, and came home. His hunger for food was so great that he could scarcely be satisfied, and notwithstanding the great quantities of food which he consumed, he became thinner and thinner, and his hunger was accompanied with great pain. Doctors could do him no good. At length he met with a skilly old man, who told him that there was an animal in his stomach, and advised him to procure a salt herring and eat it raw, and on no account to take any drink, but go at once to the side of a pool or burn and lie down there with his mouth open, and watch the result. He had not lain long when he felt something moving within him, and by and bye an ugly toad came out of his mouth, and made for the water. Having drank its fill, it was returning to its old quarters, when the old soldier rose and killed it. Many in the village had seen the dead toad. After this the man recovered rapidly. Many other stories of people swallowing *asks* (newts), and other water animals which lived in their stomachs, and produced serious diseases, were current in my young days. This gave boys a great fear of stretching down and drinking from a pool, or even a running stream.

CHAPTER VII.

THERE is another class of superstitions which have prevailed from ages the most remote to the present day, although now they are dying out—at least, they are not now employed to determine such important matters as they once were. I refer to the practice of divining, or casting lots. In early times such practices were regarded as a direct appeal to God. From the Old and New Testaments we learn that these practices were resorted to by the Jews; but in modern times, and among Western nations, the lot was regarded as an appeal to the devil as much as to God. I have known people object to the lot as a sinful practice; but, at the same time, they were in the constant habit of directing their own course by such an appeal, as, for instance, when they were about to travel on some important business, they would fix that, if certain events happened, they would regard such as a good omen from God, and would accordingly undertake their journey; but if not, they would regard the non-occurrence as an unfavourable omen, and defer their journey, in submission, as they supposed, to the will of God. In modern times, the practice of casting lots to determine legal or other important questions has been abandoned by civilized nations; but the practice still exists in less civilized communities, and is employed to determine such serious matters as involve questions of life or death, and it still survives among us in trivial matters, as games.

In my young days, a process of divining, allied to casting lots, was resorted to by young women in order to discover a thief, or to ascertain whether a young man who was courting one of them was in earnest, and would in the future become that girl's husband. The process was called the Bible and key trial, and the formula was as follows :—A key and Bible were procured, the key being so much longer than the Bible that, when placed between the leaves, the head and handle would project. If the enquiry was about the good faith of a sweetheart, the key was placed in Ruth i. 16, on the words, "Entreat me not to leave thee : where thou goest I will go," etc. The Bible was then closed, and tied round with tape. Two neutral persons, sitting opposite each other, held out the forefingers of their right hands, and the person who was consulting the oracle suspended the Bible between their two hands, resting the projecting parts of the key on the outstretched forefingers. No one spoke except the enquirer, and she, as she placed the key and Bible in position, repeated slowly the whole passage, " Entreat me not to leave thee," John or James, or whatever the name of the youth was, "for where thou goest I will go," etc. If the key and Bible turned and fell off the fingers, the answer was favourable; and generally by the time the whole passage was repeated this was the result, provided the parties holding up the key and Bible were firm and steady. For the detection of a thief, the formula was the same, with only this difference, that the key was put into the Bible at the fiftieth Psalm, and the enquirer named the suspected thief, and then repeated the eighteenth verse of that Psalm, "When thou sawest a thief then thou consentest with him," etc. If the Bible turned round and fell, it was held to be proof that the person named was the thief. This method of divining was not frequently practised, not through want of faith in its efficacy, but through superstitious terror, for the movement of the key was regarded as evidence that some unseen dread power was present, and so overpowering occasionally was the impression produced that the young woman who was chief actor in the scene fainted. The parties holding the key and Bible were generally old women, whose faith in the ordeal was perfect, and who, removed by their age from the intenser sympathies of youth, could therefore hold their hands with steadier nerve. It is only when firm hands hold it that the turning takes place, for this phenomenon depends upon the regular and steady pulsations in the fingers, and when held steadily the ordeal never fails.

There were various other methods for divining or consulting fate or deity. M'Tagart refers to a practice of divining by the staff. When a pilgrim at any time got bewildered, he would poise his staff perpendicularly, and there leave it to fall of itself; and in whatever direction it fell, that was the road he would take, believing himself supernaturally directed. Townsmen when they wished to go on a pleasure excursion to the country, and careless or unsettled which way to go, would apply to this form of lot. In the old song of " Jock Burnie " there occurs the following verse :—

" En' on en' he poised his rung, then
    Watch'd the airt its head did fa',
    Whilk was east, he lapt and sung then,
      For there his dear bade, Meg Macraw."

This practice was common with boys in the country fifty years ago, both for determining where to go for pleasure, or if in a game one of their number had hidden, and could not be found, as a last resort the stick was poised, and in whatever direction the stick fell, search was renewed in that direction.

Such things as these seem trifling, and it would seem folly to treat them seriously ; but they were not always trifling matters. Some of our Biblical scholars say that it was to this kind of divining that the prophet Hosea referred when he said, " Their staff declareth unto them," and at the present day there are nations who practice such methods for determining important affairs of life.

The New Zealand sorcerers use sticks for divining, which they throw into the air, and come to their decisions by observing in which direction these sticks fall. Even in such matters as sickness or bodily injury, the direction in which the falling sticks lie, or it may be a certain stick in the group, directs the way to a physician. In ancient times the Magian form of divining was by staves or sticks. The diviner carried with him a bundle of willow wands, and when about to divine he untied the bundle and laid the wands upon the ground ; then he gathered them and threw them from him, repeating certain words as if consulting some divinity. The wands were of different lengths, and their numbers varied from three to nine, but only the odd numbers 1, 3, 5, 7, 9 belonged to heaven, the even numbers 2, 4, 6, 8 belonged to earth.

The Chinese divine after this fashion at the present day. From such ideas has doubtless arisen the saying that there is luck in odd numbers, a belief which, after a fashion, still prevails.

The virtue and mysterious power of the divining rod is still believed by many, and has frequently been resorted to during this century for the purpose of discovering water springs and metallic veins. The diviner takes a willow wand with a forked end : the forked points are held in his two hands, the other end pointing horizontally in front of him, and as he walks slowly over a field he watches the movements of the rod. When it bends towards the earth, as if apparently strongly attracted thereto, he feels certain he is passing over a spring or metallic vein. But the phenomenon, it is believed, will not take place with every one who may try it, there being only certain parties, mediums as we would name them in these days, who have the gift of operating successfully ; and such parties obtained great fame in countries and districts where water was scarce, as they were able to point out the exact spots where wells should be dug, and also in such counties as Cornwall, where they could point out the spots where a mine could profitably be sunk. Again and again within these few years have warm controversies been carried on in public papers on the question of the reality of the virtue and power of the *dousing rod* for discovering minerals or mineral veins. Some have argued that a hazel rod is as perfect as a willow rod, and have adduced instances of its successful application.

There was another form of divining essentially an appeal to the lot, in which a stick was used, and which was frequently employed to determine matters of considerable importance. Boys resorted to it in their games in order to determine between two parties, to settle for example which side should take a certain part in a game, or which of two lads, leaders in a game, should have the first choice of associates. A long stick was thrown into the air and caught by one of the parties, then each alternately grasped it hand over hand, and he who got the last hold was the successful party. He might not have sufficient length of stick to fill his whole hand, but if by closing his hand upon the end projecting from his opponent's hand, he could support the weight of the stick, this was enough.

The various methods of divining which are generally regarded as modern inventions, such as the many forms of divining by cards, the reading of the future from the position of the leaves of tea in a tea-cup, etc., we will pass by without comment, only remarking that the prevalence among us still of such superstitious notions shows that men, notwithstanding our boasted civilisation, are still open to believe in mysteries which, to common sense, are incredible, without exhibiting the slightest trace of scepticism, and without taking any trouble to investigate the truth of the pretensions, contenting themselves with a saying I have often heard—"Wonderful things were done of old which we cannot understand, and God's hand is not yet shortened. He can do now what He did then." And so they save themselves trouble of reasoning, a process which, to the majority, is disagreeable.

CHAPTER VIII.

MANY other superstitious notions still exist among us with respect to certain animals, which have, no doubt, had their origin in remote times—some of them, doubtless, being survivals of ancient forms of animal worship. The ancient Egyptians worshipped animals, or held certain animals as symbols of divine powers. The Jews made a division of animals into clean and unclean, and the ancient Persians held certain animals in detestation as having a connection with the evil spirit; while others were esteemed by them as connected with the good spirit or principle. Other ancient nations held certain animals as more sacred than others, and these ideas still exist among us, modified and transformed to a greater or less extent. The robin is a familiar example of a bird which is held in veneration by the popular mind. The legend of the robins in the *Babes in the Wood* may have increased this veneration. There was a popular saying that the robin had a drop of God's blood in its veins, and that therefore to kill or hurt it was a sin, and that some evil would befall anyone who did so, and, conversely, any kindness done to poor robin would be repaid in some fashion. Boys did not dare to harry a robin's nest.

The *yellow yite*, or yellow hammer, was held in just the opposite estimation, and although one of the prettiest of birds, their nests were remorselessly harried, and their young often cruelly killed. When young, I was present at an act of this sort, and, as an illustration of courage and affection in the parent bird, I may relate the circumstance. The nest, with four fledglings, was about a quarter of a mile outside the village. It was carried through the village to a quarry, as far on the opposite side. The parent bird followed the boys, uttering a plaintive cry all the way. On reaching the quarry, the nest was laid on the ground, and a certain distance measured off, where the boys were to stand and throw stones at it. While this was being done, the parent bird flew to the nest, and made strenuous efforts to draw it away; and when the stones were thrown, it flew to a little distance, continuing its cry; and only flew away when it was made the mark for the stones. These boys would never have thought of doing the same thing to a nest of robins. It was said to have a drop of the devil's blood in its veins, and that its jerky and unsteady flight was a consequence of this. The hatred to the yellow hammer, however, was only local. The swallow was also considered to have a drop of the *deil's* blood in its veins; but, unlike the yellow hammer, instead of being persecuted, it was feared, and therefore let alone. If a swallow built its nest in a window-corner, it was regarded as a lucky omen, and the annoyance and filth arising therefrom was patiently borne with under the belief that such a presence brought luck and prosperity to the house. To tear down a swallow's nest was looked upon as a daring of the fates, and when this was done by the proprietor or tenant, there were many who would prophesy that death or some other great calamity would overtake, within a twelvemonth, the family of the perpetrator. To possess a hen which took to crowing like a cock boded ill to the possessor or his family if it were not disposed of either by killing or selling. They were generally sold to be killed. Only a few years ago I had such a prodigy among a flock of hens which I kept about my works, and one day it was overheard crowing, when one of the workmen came to me, and, with a solemn face, told the circumstance, and advised me strongly to have it destroyed or put away, as some evil would surely follow, relating instances he had known in Ireland. This superstition has found expression in the Scotch proverb : "Whistling maids and crowing hens are no canny about a house."

Seeing magpies before breakfast was a good or bad omen according to the number seen up to four. This was expressed in the following rhyme, which varies slightly in different localities. The following version was current in my native village :—

> " One bodes grief, two's a death,
> Three's a wedding, four's a birth."

Chambers in his Scottish Rhymes has it thus :—

> " One's joy, two's grief,
> Three's a wedding, four's a birth."

I knew a man who, if on going to his work he had seen two *piets* together, would have refrained from working before he had taken breakfast, believing that if he did so it would result in evil either to himself or his family.

If a cock crew in the morning with its head in at the door of the house, it was a token that a stranger would pay the family a visit that day; and so firm was the *faith* in this that it was often followed by works, the house being *redd* up for the occasion. I remember lately visiting an old friend in the country, and on making my appearance I was hailed with the salutation, "Come awa, I knew we would have a visit from strangers to-day, for the cock crowed thrice over with his head in at the door." If a horse stood and looked through a gateway or along a road where a bride or bridegroom dwelt, it was a very bad omen for the future happiness of the intending couple. The one dwelling in that direction would not live long.

If a bird got any human hair, and used it in building its nest, the person on whose head the hair grew would be troubled with headaches, and would very soon get bald.

It is still a common belief that crows begin to build their nests on the first Sabbath of March.

A bird coming into a house and flying over any one's head was an unlucky omen for the person over whose head it flew.

It was said that eggs laid upon Good Friday never got stale, and that butter made on that day possessed medicinal properties.

If a horse neighed at the door of a house, it boded sickness to some of the inmates.

A cricket singing on the hearth was a good omen, a token of coming riches to the family.

If a bee came up in a straight line to a person's face, it was regarded as a forerunner of important news.

If a servant wilfully killed a spider, she would certainly, it was said, break a piece of crockery or glass during that day.

Spiders were, as they are still, generally detested in a house, and were often very roughly dislodged ; but yet their lives were protected by a very old superstition. There is an old English proverb—

" If you wish to live and thrive,
Let the spider run alive."

When my mother saw a spider's web in the house she swept it away very roughly, but the spider was not wilfully killed.   If it was not seen it was considered all right, but if it fell on the floor or was seen running along the wall, it was brushed out of the room ; none of us were allowed to put our foot on it, or wilfully kill it. This care for the life of the spider is probably due to the influence of an old legend that a spider wove its web over the place where the baby Christ was hid, thus preserving his life by screening him from sight of those who sought to kill him.   Stories of a similar character are related in connection with King Robert Bruce, and several other notable persons during times of persecution, who, while hiding in caves, spiders came and wove their webs over the entrances, which, when their enemies saw, convinced them that the parties they were in search of had not taken refuge there, or the webs would have been destroyed.

The common white butterfly was a favourite with children, and to catch one and preserve it alive was considered lucky.   Care was taken to preserve them by feeding them with sugar.   But the dark brown and spotted butterflies were always detested, and were named witch butterflies.   Ill luck, it was believed, would attend any one who kept one alive, but to kill one was an unlucky transaction, which would be attended by evil to the killer before evening.

Beetles were held in aversion by most people, and if one was found upon the person, if they were at all nervous, it was sufficient to cause a fit, at least would set them screaming with a shudder of detestation.   But there was a variety of small beetles with a beautiful bronze coloured back, called *gooldies* by children, which were held in great favour.   They were sometimes kept by children as little pets, and allowed to run upon their hands and clothes, and this was not because of their beauty, but because to possess a *gooldie* was considered very lucky.   To kill a beetle brought rain the following day.

The lady bird, with its scarlet coat spotted with black, was another great favourite with most people.   Very few would kill a lady bird, as such an act would surely be followed by calamity of some sort.   Children were eager to catch one and watch it gracefully spreading out its wings from under its coat of mail, and then taking flight, while the group of youthful onlookers would repeat the rhyme,

> " Lady bird, lady bird, fly away home,
> Your house is on fire, and your children at home."

or

> " Lady lady landers, fly away to Flanders."

But these practices were not altogether confined to children.   Grown up girls, when they caught a lady bird, held it in their hands, and repeated the following couplet—

> " Fly away east or fly away west,
> And show me where lives the one I like best."

Its flight was watched with great anxiety, and when it took the direction which the young girl wished, it was not only a sort of pleasure, but a proof of the augury.

If a person on going to his work, or while going an errand, were to see a hare cross the road in front of him, it was a token that ill luck would shortly befall him. Many under such circumstances would return home and not pursue their quest until the next meal had been eaten, for beyond that the evil influence did not extend.   This superstition is very old, but it is not in every country or age connected with the hare.   We have already seen in a quotation from Ovid that this superstition existed in his day, (page 2.)   Probably the hare has been adopted in this country from the belief that witches assumed the form of that animal when on their nightly rambles, for how was the wayfarer to know that the hare which he saw was not a transformed witch, intent on working him mischief?

The cat was always a favourite in a family, and nothing was more unlucky than for one to die inside the house. I have known cases where, when such a misfortune occurred, the family were thrown into great consternation, surmising what possible form of evil this omen portended to them.   Generally when a cat was known to be ailing, the animal was removed from the house and placed in the coal cellar, or other outhouse, with plenty of food, and kept there until it either recovered or died. With the ancient Egyptians the cat was one of their favourite animals. The death of a cat belonging to a family was considered a great misfortune. Upon the oocurrence of such an event the household went into mourning, shaving off their eyebrows, and otherwise indicating their sorrow. In Scotland it was believed that witches often assumed the cat form while exercising their evil influence over a family.

It was pretty generally believed a few years ago that in large fires kept continually burning there was generated an animal called a salamander. It required seven years to grow and attain maturity, and if the fires were kept burning longer than that there was great danger that the animal might make its escape from its fiery matrix, and, if this should happen, it would range round the world, destroying all it came in contact with, itself almost in-destructible. Hence large fires, such as those of blast furnaces in ironworks, were extinguished before the ex-piry of the seven years, and the embryo monster taken out. Such an idea may have had its origin in a misin-terpretation of some of St. John's apocalyptic visions, or may have been a survival of the legend of the fiery dragon whose very breath was fire, a legend common during the middle ages and also in ancient Rome. Bacon, in his *Natural History*, says—"There is an ancient tradition of the salamander that it liveth in the fire, and hath force also to extinguish the fire"; and, according to Pliny, Book X. chap. 67,—"The sala-mander, made in fashion of a lizard, with spots like to stars, never comes abroad, and sheweth itself only during great showers. In fair weather, he is not seen; he is of so cold a complexion that if he do but touch the fire he would quench it."—*Holland.* This is quite opposite to the modern notion of it that it was generated in the fire, but such legends take transformations suitable to the age and locality.

The goat has been associated both in ancient and modern times with the devil, or evil spirit, who is depicted with horns, hoofs, and a tail. In modern times, he was supposed to haunt streams and woods in this disguise, and to be present at many social gatherings. He was popularly credited with assisting, in this disguise, in the instruction of a novice into the mysteries of Freemasonry, and was supposed to allow the novice to ride on his back, and go withershins three times round the room. I have known men who were anxious to be admitted into the order deterred by the thought of thus meeting with the devil at their initiation.

While staying at Luss lately, I was informed that a mill near to Loch Lomond had formerly been haunted by the goat demon, and that the miller had suffered much from its mischievous disposition. It frequently let on the water when there was no grain to grind. But one night the miller watched his mill, and had a meeting with the goblin, who demanded the miller's name, and was informed that it was *myself.* After a trial of strength, the miller got the best of it, and the spirit departed. After hearing this, I remembered that the same story, under a slightly-different form, had been told me when a boy in my native village. This was the story as then told :—A certain miller in the west missed a quantity of his meal every day, although his mill was carefully and

securely locked.   One night he sat up and watched,
hiding himself behind the hopper.   After a time, he was
surprised to see the hopper beginning to go, and, looking
up, he saw a little manakin holding a little cappie in his
hand and filling it at the hopper.   The miller was so
frightened that this time he let him go; but, in a few
minutes, the manakin returned again with his cappie.
Then the miller stepped out from his hiding-place, and
said, "Aye, my manakin, and wha may you be, and
what's your name?"   To which the manakin, without
being apparently disturbed, replied, "My name is Self,
and what's your name?"   "My name is Self, too,"
replied the miller.   The manakin's cappie being by
this time again full, he began to walk off, but the miller
gave him a whack with his stick, and then ran again to
his hiding-place.   The manakin gave a terrible yell,
which brought from a hidden corner an old woman, crying, "Wha did it?   Wha did it?"   The manakin
answered, "It was Self did it."   Whereat, slapping the
manakin on the cheek, the old woman said, "If Self
did it, Self must mend it again."   After this, they both
left the mill, which immediately stopped working.   The
miller was never afterwards troubled in this way, and, at
the same time, a goat which for generations had been
observed at gloaming and on moonlight nights in the
dell, and on the banks of the stream which drove the
mill, disappeared, and was never seen again.

To meet a sow the first thing in the morning boded
bad luck for the day.

If a male cat came into the house and shewed itself
friendly to any one, it was a lucky omen for that person.

To meet a piebald horse was lucky.   If two such

horses were met apart, the one after the other, and if then the person who met them were to spit three times, and express any reasonable wish, it would be granted within three days.

If a stray dog followed any person on the street, without having been enticed, it was lucky, and success was certain to attend the errand on which the person was engaged.

CHAPTER IX.

SUPERSTITIONS connected with plants were more numerous than those connected with animals. We have already noticed wide-spread prevalence of tree worship in early times. The Bible is full of evidence bearing upon this point, from the earliest period of Jewish history until the time of the captivity. Even concerning those Kings of Judah and Israel who are recorded to have walked in the ways of their father David, it is frequently remarked of them that they did not remove or hew down the *groves*, but permitted them to remain a snare to the people. In several instances the word translated grove cannot pro-perly be applicable to a grove of trees, but must signify something much smaller, for it is in these instances des-cribed as being located in the temple. It can therefore refer only to a tree or stump of a tree, or it may be only the symbol of a tree. The story of the tree of good and evil, and the tree of life, has been the origin of many superstitious notions regarding trees. The notion that the tree of the knowledge of good and evil was an apple tree, caused the apple to have a great many mystic mean-ings, and gave it a prominent place in many legends, and also brought it into prominence as a divining medium. In many parts of Scotland the apple was believed to have great influence in love affairs.   If an apple seed were shot between the fingers it was understood that it would, by the direction of its flight, indicate the direction from which that person's future partner in life would come. If a couple took an apple on St. John's eve and cut it in two, and if the seeds on each half were found to be equal in number, this was a token that these two would be soon united in marriage ; or if the halves contained an unequal number of seeds, the one who possessed the half with the greater number would be married first.   If a seed were cut in two, it denoted trouble to the party holding the larger portion of the seed.   If two seeds were cut, it denoted early death or widowhood to one of the parties. If the apple were sour or sweet, the flavour indicated the temper of the parties.   There was a practice common among young people of peeling an apple in an unbroken peel, and throwing the peeled skin over the right shoulder in order to ascertain from the manner in which it fell, first, whether the person who threw it would be married soon, and second, the trade or profession of the person to whom they would be married.   If the skin after being thrown remained unbroken, they would be married soon, and the person to whom they would be married was ascertained from the form which the fallen skin presented ; this form might assume the shape of a letter, in that case it was the initial letter of the unknown parties name, or it might assume the form of some trade tool, &c.   Imagination had free scope here.   The apple tree itself was considered a lucky tree to have near a house, but its principal virtue lay in the fruit.

Holly.   This name is probably a corruption of the word holy, as this plant has been used from time immemorial as a protection against evil influence. It was hung round, or planted near houses, as a protection against lightning. Its common use at Christmas is apparently the survival of an ancient Roman custom, occurring during the festival to Saturn, to which god the holly was dedicated. While the Romans were holding this feast, which occurred about the time of the winter solstice, they decked the outsides of their houses with holly; at the same time the Christians were quietly celebrating the birth of Christ, and to avoid detection they outwardly followed the custom of their· heathen neighbours, and decked their houses with holly also. In this way the holly came to be connected with our Christmas customs. (See chapter on Festivals.) This plant was also regarded as a symbol of the resurrection. The use of mistletoe along with holly is probably due to the notion that in winter the fairies took shelter under its leaves, and that they protected all who sheltered the plant. The origin of kissing under the mistletoe is considered to have come from our Saxon ancestors, who regarded this plant as dedicated to *Friga*, the goddess of love.

The *Aspen* was said to have been the tree on which Judas hanged himself after the betrayal of his Master, and ever since its leaves have trembled with shame.

The *Ash* had wonderful influence. The old Christmas log was of ash wood, and the use of it at this time was helpful to the future prosperity of the family. Venomous animals, it was said, would not take shelter under its branches. A carriage with its axles made of ash wood was believed to go faster than a carriage with its axles made of any other wood; and tools with handles made of this wood were supposed to enable a man to do more work than he could do with tools whose handles were not of ash. Hence the reason that ash wood is generally used for tool handles. It was upon ash branches that witches were enabled to ride through the air; and those who ate on St. John's eve the red buds of the tree, were rendered invulnerable to witch influence.

The *Hazel* was dedicated to the god *Thor*, and, in the Roman Catholic Church, was esteemed a plant of great virtue for the cure of fevers. When used as a divining rod, the rod, if it were cut on St. John's Day or Good Friday, would be certain to be a successful instrument of divination. A hazel rod was a badge of authority, and it was probably this notion which caused it to be made use of by school masters. Among the Romans, a hazel rod was also a symbol of authority.

The *Willow*, as might be expected, had many superstitious notions connected with it, since, according to the authorized version of the English Bible, the Israelites are said to have hung their harps on willow trees. The weeping willow is said to have, ever since the time of the Jews' captivity in Babylon, drooped its branches, in sympathy with this circumstance. The common willow was held to be under the protection of the devil, and it was said that, if any were to cast a knot upon a young willow, and sit under it, and thereupon renounce his or her baptism, the devil would confer upon them supernatural power.

The *Elder*, or *Bourtree*, had wonderful influence as a protection against evil. Wherever it grew, witches were powerless. In this country, gardens were protected by having elder trees planted at the entrance, and sometimes hedges of this plant were trained round the garden. There are very few old gardens in country places in which are not still seen remains of the protecting elder tree. In my boyhood, I remember that my brothers, sisters, and myself were warned against breaking a twig or branch from the elder hedge which surrounded my grandfather's garden. We were told at the time, as a reason for this prohibition, that it was poisonous; but we discovered afterwards that there was another reason, viz., that it was unlucky to break off even a small twig from a bourtree bush. In some parts of the Continent this superstitious feeling is so strong that, before pruning it, the gardener says—"Elder, elder, may I cut thy branches?" If no response be heard, it is considered that assent has been given, and then, after spitting three times, the pruner begins his cutting. According to Montanus, elder wood formed a portion of the fuel used in the burning of human bodies as a protection against evil influences; and, within my own recollection, the driver of a hearse had his whip handle made of elder wood for a similar reason. In some parts of Scotland, people would not put a piece of elder wood into the fire, and I have seen, not many years ago, pieces of this wood lying about unused, when the neighbourhood was in great straits for firewood; but none would use it, and when asked why? the answer was—"We don't know, but folks say it is not lucky to burn the bourtree." It was believed that children laid in a cradle made in whole or in part of elderwood, would not sleep well, and were in danger of falling out of the cradle. Elder berries, gathered on St. John's Eve, would prevent the possessor suffering from witchcraft, and often bestowed

upon their owners magical powers.   If the elder were
planted in the form of a cross upon a new-made grave,
and if it bloomed, it was a sure sign that the soul of the
dead person was happy.

The *Onion* was regarded as a symbol of the universe
among the ancient Egyptians, and many curious beliefs
were associated with it.   It was believed by them that it
attracted and absorbed infectious matters, and was
usually hung up in rooms to prevent maladies.   This
belief in the absorptive virtue of the onion is prevalent
even at the present day.   When a youth, I remember
the following story being told, and implicitly believed
by all.   There was once a certain king or nobleman
who was in want of a physician, and two celebrated
doctors applied.   As both could not obtain the situation,
they agreed among themselves that the one was to try
to poison the other, and he who succeeded in
overcoming the poison would thus be left free to fill the
situation.   They drew lots as to who should first take
the poison.   The first dose given was a stewed toad, but
the party who took it immediately applied a poultice of
peeled onions over his stomach, and thus abstracted all
the poison of the toad.   Two days after, the other doctor
was given the onions to eat.   He ate them, and died.
It was generally believed that a poultice of peeled onions
laid on the stomach, or underneath the armpits, would
cure any one who had taken poison.   My mother would
never use onions which had lain for any length of time
with their skins off.

So lately as 1849, Mr. J. B. Wolff, in the *Scientific
American*, states that he had charge of one hundred
men on shipboard, cholera raging among them; they

had onions on board, which a number of the men freely ate, and these were soon attacked by the cholera and nearly all died. As soon as this discovery was made, the eating of the onions was forbidden. Mr. Wolff came to the conclusion that onions should never be eaten during an epidemic; he remarks, "After many years experience, I have found that onions placed in a room where there is small-pox, will blister and decompose with great rapidity,—not only so, but will prevent the spread of disease;" and he thinks that, as a disinfectant, they have no equal, only keep them out of the stomach.

It was believed that, when peeling onions, if an onion were stuck on the point of the knife which was being used, it would prevent the eyes being affected.

The common *Fern*, it was believed, was in flower at midnight on St. John's Eve, and whoever got possession of the flower would be protected from all evil influences, and would obtain a revelation of hidden treasure.

St.-John's-Wort. In heathen mythology the summer solstice was a day dedicated to the sun, and was believed to be a day on which witches held their festivities. St.-John's-Wort was their symbolical plant, and people were won't to judge from it whether their future would be lucky or unlucky ; as it grew they read in its progressive character their future lot. The Christians dedicated this festive period to St. John the Baptist, and the sacred plant was named St.-John's-Wort or root, and became a talisman against evil. In one of the old romantic ballads a young lady falls in love with a demon, who tells her

" Gin you wish to be Leman mine,
Lay aside the St.-John's-wort and the vervain. "

When hung up on St. John's day together with a cross over the doors of houses it kept out the devil and other evil spirits. To gather the root on St. John's day morning at sunrise, and retain it in the house, gave luck to the family in their undertakings, especially in those begun on that day. Plants with *lady* attached to their names were in ancient times dedicated to some goddess ; and in Christian times the term was transferred to the Virgin Mary. Such plants have good qualities, conferring protection and favour on their possessors.

From the earliest times the *Rose* has been an emblem of silence. *Eros*, in the Greek mythology, presents a rose to the god of silence, and to this day *sub rosa*, or "under the rose," means the keeping of a secret. Roses were used in very early times as a potent ingredient in love philters. In Greece it was customary to leave bequests for the maintenance of rose gardens, a custom which has come down to recent times. Rose gardens were common during the middle ages. According to Indian mythology, one of the wives of Vishna was found in a rose. In Rome it was the custom to bless the rose on a certain Sunday, called *Rose Sunday*. The custom of blessing the golden rose came into vogue about the eleventh century. The golden rose thus consecrated was given to princes as a mark of the Roman Pontifs' favour. In the east it is still believed that the first rose was generated by a tear of the prophet Mahomet, and it is further believed that on a certain day in the year the rose has a heart of gold. In the West of Scotland if a white rose bloomed in autumn it was a token of early death to some one, but if a red rose did the same, it was a token of an early marriage. The red rose, it was said, would not bloom over a grave. If a young girl had several lovers, and wished to know which of them would be her husband, she would take a rose leaf for each of her sweethearts, and naming each leaf after the name of one of her lovers, she would watch them till one after another they sank, and the last to sink would be her future husband. Rose leaves thrown upon a fire gave good luck. If a rose bush were pruned on St. John's eve, it would bloom again in the autumn. Superstitions respecting the rose are more numerous in England than in Scotland.

The *Lily* had a sacredness associated with it, probably on account of Christ's reference to it. It was employed as a charm against evil influence, and as an antidote to love philters; but I am not aware of any of these uses being put in practice during this century.

The four-leaved *Clover* had extraordinary influence in preserving its possessor from magical and witch influence, and enabled their possessors also to see through any deceit or device which might be tried against them. I have seen a group of young women within these few years searching eagerly for this charmed plant.

The *Oak*, from time immemorial, has held a high place as a sacred tree. The Druids worshipped the oak, and performed many of their rites under the shadow of its branches. When Augustine preached Christianity to the ancient Britons, he stood under an oak tree. The ancient Hebrews evidently held the oak as a sacred tree. There is a tradition that Abraham received his heavenly visitors under an oak. Rebekah's nurse was buried under an oak, called afterwards the oak of weeping. Jacob buried the idols of Shechem under an oak. It was under the oak of Ophra, Gideon saw the angel sitting, who gave him instructions as to what he was to do to free Israel. When Joshua and Israel made a covenant to serve God, a great stone was set up in evidence under an oak that was by the sanctuary of the Lord. The prophet sent to prophesy against Jeroboam was found at Bethel sitting under an oak. Saul and his sons were buried under an oak, and, according to Isaiah, idols were made of oak wood. Abimelech was made king by the oak that was in Shechem. From these proofs we need not be surprised that the oak continued to be held in veneration, and was believed to possess virtues overcoming evil. During last century its influence in curing diseases was believed in. The toothache could be cured by boring with a nail the tooth or gum till blood came, and then driving the nail into an oak tree. A child with rupture could be cured by splitting an oak branch, and passing the child through the opening backwards three times ; if the splits grew together afterwards, the child would be cured. The same was believed in as to the ash tree. In the Presbytery Records of Lanark, 1664 :—" Compeirs Margaret Reid in the same parish, (Carnwath), suspect of witchcraft, and confessed she put a woman newlie delivered, thrice through a green halshe, for helping a grinding of the bellie ; and that she carried a sick child thrice about ane aikine post for curing of it." Such means of curing diseases were practised within this century, and many things connected with the oak were held potent as curatives.

CHAPTER X.

GLAMOUR was a kind of witch power which certain people were supposed to be gifted with ; by the exercise of such influence they took command over their subjects' sense of sight, and caused them to see whatever they desired that they should see. Sir Walter Scott describes the recognised capability of glamour power in the following lines :—

> " It had much of glamour might,
> Could make a lady seem a knight,
> The cobwebs on a dungeon wall,
> Seem tapestry in lordly hall.
> A nutshell seem a gilded barge,
> A sheeling seem a palace large,
> And youth seem age, and age seem youth,
> All was delusion, nought was truth."

Gipsies were believed to possess this power, and for their own ends to exercise it over people. In the ballad of " Johnny Faa," Johnny is represented as exercising this power over the Countess of Cassillis—

> " And she came tripping down the stairs,
> With a' her maids before her,
> And soon as he saw her weel faured face,
> He coost the glamour o'er her."

To possess a four-leaved clover completely protected any one from this power. I remember a story which I heard when a boy, and the narrator of it I recollect spoke as if he were quite familiar with the fact. A certain man came to the village to exhibit the strength of a wonderful cock, which could draw, when attached to its leg by a rope, a large log of wood. Many people went and paid to see this wonderful performance, which was exhibited in the back yard of a public house. One of the spectators present on one occasion had in his possession a four-leaved clover, and while others saw, as they supposed, a log of wood drawn through the yard, this person saw only a straw attached to the cock's leg by a small thread. I may mention here that the four-leaved clover was reputed to be a preventative against madness, and against being drafted for military service.

One very ancient and persistent superstition had regard to the direction of movement either of persons or things. This direction should always be with the course of the sun. To move against the sun was improper and productive of evil consequences, and the name given to this direction of movement was *withershins*. Witches in their dances and other pranks, always, it was said, went *withershins*. Mr. Simpson in his work, *Meeting the Sun*, says, "The Llama monk whirls his praying cylinder in the way of the sun, and fears lest a stranger should get at it and turn it contrary, which would take from it all the virtue it had acquired. They also build piles of stone, and always pass them on one side, and return on the other, so as to make a circuit with the sun. Mahommedans make the circuit of the Caaba in the same way. The ancient dagobas of India and Ceylon were also traversed round in the same way, and the old Irish and Scotch custom is to make all move-

ments *Deisual,* or sunwise, round houses and graves,
and to turn their bodies in this way at the beginning
and end of a journey for luck, as well as at weddings
and other ceremonies."

To go *withershins* and to read prayers or the creed
backwards were great evils, and pointed to connection
with the devil. The author of *Olrig Grange,* in an early
poem, sketches this superstition very graphically :—

> " Hech ! sirs, but we had grand fun
> Wi' the meikle black deil in the chair,
> And the muckle Bible upside doon
> A' ganging withershins roun and roun,
> And backwards saying the prayer
> About the warlock's grave,
> Withershins ganging roun ;
> And kimmer and carline had for licht
> The fat o' a bairn they buried that nicht,
> Unchristen'd, beneath the moon."

If a tree or plant grew with a twist contrary to the direction of the sun's movement, that portion was considered to possess certain powers, which are referred to in
the following verse of an old song :—

> " I'll gar my ain Tammy gae doun to the Howe
> And cut me a rock of the widdershins grow,
> Of good rantree for to carry my tow,
> And a spindle of the same for the twining o't."

Pennant refers to some other practices in Scotland in
his day, that were no doubt survivals of ancient heathen
worship. Such as on certain occasions kindling a fire,
and the people joining hands and dancing three times
round it south-ways, or according to the course of the

sun. At baptisms and marriages they walked three times round the church sun-ways. The Highlanders, in going to bathe or drink in a consecrated fountain, approach it by going round the place from east to west on the south side. When the dead are laid in their grave, the grave is approached by going round in the same manner. The bride is conducted to the spouse in presence of the minister round the company in the same direction; indeed, all public matters were done according to certain fixed ideas in relation to the sun, all pointing to a lingering ray of sun worship.

If a fire were slow or *dour* to kindle, the poker was taken and placed in front of the grate, one end resting on the fender, the other on the front bar of the grate, and this, it was believed, would cause the fire to kindle quickly. This practice is still followed by many, but being compelled now to give an apparently scientific reason for their conduct, they say that it is so placed to produce a draught. But this it does not do. The practice originated in the belief that the slow or dour fire was spell-bound by witchcraft, and the poker was so placed that it would form the shape of a cross with the front bar of the grate, and thus the witch power be destroyed. In early times when the poker was placed in this position, the person who placed it repeated an *Ave Marie* or *Paternoster*, but this feature of the ceremony died out, and with it the reason for the practice was forgotten. I have seen it done in private houses, and very frequently in the public rooms of country inns. Indeed, in such public rooms it was the common practice when the servant put on a fire, that after sweeping up the dust she placed the poker in this position, and left the room.

Probably she had no idea why she did it, but merely followed the custom.

In a general chapter, such as this, I can find room for some things which could not properly find a place in other chapters. The subject of omens has by no means been exhausted. The late George Smith, in his work upon the Chaldean Account of Genesis, says that in ancient Babylonia, 1600 B.C., everything in nature was supposed to portend some coming event. Without much exaggeration, the same might be said of the people of this country during the earlier part of this century.

On seeing the first plough in the season, it was lucky if it were seen coming towards the observer, and he or she, in whatever undertaking then engaged, might be certain of success in it; but, if seen going from the observer, the omen was reversed.

If a farmer's cows became restive without any apparent cause, it foreboded trouble to either master or mistress.

On going on any business, if the first person met with was plain-soled, the journey might be given up, for, if proceeded with, the business to be transacted would prove a failure; but, by turning and entering the house again, with the right foot first, and then partaking of food before resuming the journey, it might be undertaken without misgiving.

It was unlucky to walk under a ladder set up against a wall, but if passing under it could not be avoided, then, if before doing so, you wished for anything, your wish would be fulfilled.

It was unlucky to eat twin nuts found in one shell.

If the eye or nose itched, it was a sign that the person so affected would be vexed in some way that day. If the foot itched, it was a sign that the owner of the foot was about to undertake a strange journey. If the elbow itched, it betokened the coming of a strange bedfellow. If the right hand itched, it signified that money would shortly be received by it; and, if the left hand itched, that money would shortly have to be paid away.

If the ear tingled, it was a sign that some one was speaking of the person so affected. If it were the right ear which did so, then the speech was favourable; if the left ear, the reverse. In this latter case, if the persons whose ears tingled were to bite their little fingers, this would cause the persons speaking evil of them to bite their tongues.

To break a looking-glass, hanging against a wall, was a sign that death would shortly occur in the family.

If a daughter's petticoat was longer than her frock, it shewed that her father loved her better than her mother did.

If you desired luck with any article of dress, it should be worn first at church.

If a person unwittingly put on an article of dress outside in, it was an omen that he or she would succeed in what they undertook that day; but it was requisite that this portion of dress should remain with the wrong side out until night, for, if reversed earlier, the luck was reversed also.

To weigh children was considered an objectionable practice, as it was believed to injure their health, and cause them to grow up weakly.

If a child cut the upper teeth before the lower, it was very unlucky for the child.

If a cradle were rocked when the child was not in it,

it was said to give the child a headache; but if it so happened that the child was too old to be rocked in a cradle, but its baby clothes were still in the house, then this incident portended that its mother would have another baby.

To make a present of a knife or a pair of scissors, and refuse to accept anything in return, was said to cut or sever friendship between giver and receiver.

If, at a social gathering, a bachelor or maid were placed inadvertently betwixt a man and his wife, the person so seated would be married within a year.

If a person in rising from table overturned his chair, this shewed that he had been speaking untruths.

To feel a cold tremor along the spine was a sign that some one was treading on the spot of earth in which the person so affected would be buried.

If a person spoke aloud to himself, it was a sign that he would meet with a violent death.

If a girl married a man the initial letter of whose name was the same as her own, it was held that the union would not be a happy one. This notion was formulated into this proverb—

> " To change the name and not the letter,
> Is a change for the worse, and not for the better."

If thirteen people sat down to dinner, the first who rose from table would, it was said, either die or meet with some terrible calamity within a year's time.

When burning caking coal it often happens that a small piece of fused matter is projected from the fire. When this took place the piece was searched for and

examined, and from its shape certain events were prog-
nosticated concerning the person in whose direction it
had fallen.   If shaped like a coffin it presaged death, if
like a cradle it foretold a birth.   I have seen such an
incident produce a considerable sensation among a group
sitting round a fire.

To find the shoe of a horse and hang it behind the
house door was considered to bring good luck to
the household, and protection from witchcraft or evil
eye.   I have seen this charm in large beer shops in Lon-
don, and I was present in the parlour of one of these
beer shops when an animated discussion arose as to
whether it was most effective to have the shoe nailed behind the door, or upon the first step of the door.   Each
position had its advocates, and instances of extraordinary
luck were recounted as having attended each position.

If a youth sat musing and intently looking into the
fire, it was a sign that some one was throwing an evil
spell over him, or fascinating him for evil.   When this
was observed, if any one without speaking were to take
the tongs and turn the centre coal or piece of wood in the
grate right over, and while doing so say, " *Gude preserve us
frae a' skaith*," it would break the spell, and cause the intended evil to revert on the evil-disposed person who was
working the spell.   I have not only seen the operation performed many times, but have had it performed in my own
favour by my worthy grandmother, whose belief in such
things could never be shaken.

If the nails of a child were cut before it was a year old,
the chances were that it would grow up a thief.

To spill salt while handing it to any one was unlucky,
a sign of an impending quarrel between the parties ; but

if the person who spilled the salt carefully lifted it up with the blade of a knife, and cast it over his or her shoulder, all evil consequences were prevented. In Leonardo de Vinci's celebrated painting of the Last Supper, the painter has indicated the enmity of Judas by representing him in the act of upsetting the salt dish, with the right hand resting on the table, grasping the bag.

If a double ear of corn were put over the looking glass, it prevented the house from being struck by lightning. I have seen corn stalks hung over a looking glass, and was told that it brought luck.

It was customary for farmers to leave a portion of their fields uncropped, which was a dedication to the evil spirit, and called good man's croft. The Church exerted itself for a long time to abolish this practice, but farmers, who are generally very superstitious, were afraid to discontinue the practice for fear of ill luck. I remember a farmer as late as 1825 always leaving a small piece of a field uncropped, but then did not know why. At length he gave the right of working these bits to a poor labourer, who did well with it, and in a few years the farmer cultivated the whole himself.

Water that had been used in baptism was believed to have virtue to cure many distempers. It was a preventive against witchcraft, and eyes bathed with it would never see a ghost.

To see a dot of soot hanging on the bars of the grate indicated a visit from a stranger. By clapping the hands close to it, if the current produced by this, blew it off at the first clap, the stranger would visit that day. Every clap indicated the day before the visit would be made. This is still a common practice, of which the following

lines taken from *Glasgow Weekly Herald*, 1877, is a
graphic illustration :—

> " *Rab*—
> Eh ! Willie, come your wa's, and peace be wi' ye ;
> Wi' a' my heart, I'm truly glad to see ye.
> Wee Geordie, wha sat gazing in the fire,
> In that prophetic mood I oft admire,
> Declar'd he saw a stranger on the grate —
> And Geordie's auguries are true as fate.
> He gied his hands a clap wi' a' his micht,
> And said that stranger's coming here the nicht,
> Wi' the first clap it's off. Ye see how true
> Appears the future on wee Geordie's view.
> What's in the wind, or what may be the news,
> That brings ye here, in heedless waste o' shoes ?"

An eclipse of the sun was looked on as an omen of
coming calamity. This is a very ancient superstition,
and remained with us to a very late date, if it is even
yet extinct. In 1597, during an eclipse of the sun, it is
stated by Calderwood that men and women thought the
day of judgment was come. Many women swooned, the
streets of Edinburgh was full of crying, and in fear some
ran to the kirk to pray. I remember an eclipse about
1818, when about three parts of the sun was covered.
The alarm in the village was very great, indoor work was
suspended for the time, and in several families prayers
were offered for protection, believing that it portended
some awful calamity ; but when it passed off there was a
general feeling of relief.

Fishers on the West Coast believe that were they to
set their nets so that in any way it would encroach
upon the Sabbath, the herrings would leave the district.
Two years ago I was told that herrings were very plenti-
ful at one time at Lamlash, but some thoughtless person

set his net on a Sabbath evening.   He caught none, and
the herrings left and never returned.

I know several persons who refuse to have their likeness taken lest it prove unlucky; and give as instances
the cases of several of their friends who never had a day's
health after being photographed.

In addition to the many forms of superstition which
we have been recalling, there were, and still are a great
many superstitions connected with the phenomenon of
dreaming, but as the notions in this series were very
varied, differing very much in different localities, and
everywhere subject less or more to the fancy of the inter-
preter, and as I believe that the notions and practices
now in vogue in this connection are of comparatively
recent origin, I will not enter upon the subject.

APPENDIX.

APPENDIX.

YULE, BELTANE, & HALLOWEEN FESTIVALS:

Survivals of Ancient Sun and Fire Worship.

ISTORY and prehistoric investigations have shown quite clearly that prehistoric man worshipped the Sun, the giver and vivifier of all life, as the supreme God. To the sun they offered sacrifices, and at stated periods celebrated festivals in his honour; and at these festivals bread and wine and meat were partaken of, with observances very similar in many respects to the practices of the Jews during their religious feasts. But although the sun was the supreme deity, other objects were also worshipped as subordinate deities. These objects, however, were generally in some manner representative of sun attributes; for example, the Moon was worshipped as the spouse of the Sun, Venus as his page. The pleiades and other constellations, and single stars were also deified; the rainbow and the lightning were sun servants, the elements, the sun's offspring. Many animals and trees were reverenced as representatives of sun attributes. Above all, fire was worshipped as the truest symbol of the sun upon earth, and all offerings and sacrifices in honour of the sun were presented through fire; thus sun and fire worship became identified.

T

In Britain sun-worship appears to have been purer in prehistoric than it afterwards was in historic times, purer also than the sun-cult of historic Egypt, Greece, or Rome ; that is, there appears to have been in British sun-worship less of polytheism than prevailed in Egypt, Greece, or Rome. But during the historic period, the numerous invasions and the colonizations of different portions of this country by the Romans and other nations, who brought with them their special religious beliefs and formulæ of worship, caused the increase of polytheism by the commingling of the foreign and native elements of belief, and later on, these were mixed with Christianity, and in these mixings all the elements became modified, so that now it is very difficult to separate with certainty the aboriginal, invasional, and Christian elements.

From many indications it seems more than probable that the sun-cult in prehistoric Britain was very similar, even in many minor points, to the solar worship of the ancient Peruvians. At the same time, there is not the slightest probability that these two widely separated sun-cults ever had a common point of historical connection, nor, in order to explain their similarities, is such an historical explanation necessary. Quite sufficient is the explanation that both possessed in common a human nature, emotional and intellectual, moving on the same plane of childlike intelligence, and that both from this common standpoint had regard to the same striking and regularly recurring scenes of natural phenomena. Prescott thus describes the worship of these ancient Peruvians :—"The Sun was their primary God ; to it was built a vast temple in the capital, more radiant with gold than that of Solomon's ; and every city had a

temple dedicated to the sun, and blasphemy against
the sun was punished with death. The principal festivals of the year were at the equinoxes and solstices.
That at midsummer was the grandest. It was preceded
by a three days' fast; then every one who had time and
money visited the city. Great fires were kindled from
the sun's rays or by friction, from which sacred fires
people kindled their hearth;" all household fires having previously been extinguished. Poor countries and
districts, where the arts were in a backward condition,
instead of having temples like the Peruvians, dedicated
mountains and stone circles to the great luminary. It
is the all but universal opinion that in this country, centuries before the Christian era, the religion of the people
was Druidism; but this is merely the name of a system,
and is equivalent to our saying that the present religion
of our country is Presbyterianism, a statement which
conveys no idea of the nature of our religious worship.
The Druids were a priestly order who governed the country, and directed the worship of the people, the principal
objects of worship being, as we have already said, the
sun and fire. "The Druids," says the late Rev. James
Rust, "formed an ecclesiastico-political association, and
professed to explain the deep mysteries respecting God
and man, and were the sacerdotal rulers, and called in
consequence Druids or mystery-keepers. They were
not allowed to commit anything to writing respecting
their mysteries, and no one was allowed to enter their
order till after a prolonged probation, terminating in
swearing most solemnly to keep their mysteries secret
for ever; and by this means they obtained great power
and influence over all classes of the people."

Concerning the name Druid, the writer in the *Ency-clopedia Metropolitana* says, "The name Druid is derived from *deru*, an oak." The Druids were an order of priests; they were divided into three classes, resembling the Persian magi. The first class were the Druids proper; they were the highest nobility, to whom was entrusted all religious rites and education. The second class were the bards; they were principally employed in public instruction, which was given in verse. The third class was called *Euvates;* whose office it was to deliver the responses of the oracles, and to attend the people who consulted them. The knowledge of astronomy and computation of time possessed by the Druids was of a high order, and, no doubt, was the form of worship imported from Chaldea.

It is known that the Phœnicians had colonized Britain at least 1000 years B.C., and doubtless they would bring with them their form of worship, their gods being the sun, the moon, and fire. We may here find a very early source for the institution of sun-worship in these islands, if we can believe that such a very partial colonization as was effected by the Phœnicians could work a religious similarity throughout the entire island. I think it probable that sun-worship existed before the Phœnicians came to the island, but they may have elevated its practice. Following the writer in the *Encyclopedia Metropolitana*, we are told that in addition to their worship of the sun, the Druids "held sacred the spirits of their ancestors, paid great honour to mountains, lakes, and groves. Groves of oak were their temples, and their places of worship were open to heaven, such as stone circles. They had also a ceremony of baptism, dipping in the sacred lake, as an initiatory rite, and had also a sacrament of bread and wine. They paid great reverence to the egg of the serpent, the seed of the oak, and above all, the mistletoe that grew upon the oak ; and they offered in sacrifice to the sun and fire, men and animals."

Many of the localities where their worship was observed in this country can still be identified through the names which these places still bear. One or two are here given, because they refer to sun-worship :—

Grenach (in Perthshire), means *Field of the Sun*.

Greenan (a stream in Perthshire), means *River of the Sun*.

Balgreen (a town in Perthshire and other counties), means *Town of the Sun*.

Grian chnox (Greenock), means *Knoll of the Sun*.

Granton, means *Sun's Fire*.

Premising, therefore, that sun-worship and Druidical customs form the original base of all our old national festivals, we will now direct attention to the great festival of

YULE.

The term *Yule* was the name given to the festival of the winter solstice by our northern invaders, and means *the Festival of the Sun*. One of the names by which the Scandinavians designated the sun was *Julvatter*, meaning *Yule-father* or *Sun-father*. In Saxon the festival was called *Gehul*, meaning *Sun-feast*. In Danish it is *Juul*; in Swedish *Oel*. Chambers supposes that the name is from a root word meaning *wheel*. We have no trace of the name by which the Druids knew this feast. The

Rev. Mr. Smiddy in his book on *Druidism in Ireland*, says, " Their great feast was that called in the Irish tongue *Nuadhulig*, meaning *new all heal*, or new mistletoe. When the day came the priests assembled outside the town, and the people gathered shouting *all heal*. Then began a solemn procession into the forests in search of the mistletoe growing on the favourite oak. When found, the priests ascended the tree, and cut down the divine plant with a golden knife, which was secured below upon a linen cloth of spotless white; two white bulls were then conducted to the spot for the occasion, and there sacrificed to the sun god. The plant was then brought home with shouts of joy, mingled with prayers and hymns, and then followed a general religious feast, and afterwards scenes of boisterous merriment, to which all were admitted."

From other accounts of this sun feast at the winter solstice in this country, we are given to understand that besides white bulls there were also human victims offered in sacrifice. The mistletoe gathered was divided among the people, who hung the sprays over their doorways as a protection from evil influences, and as a propitiation to the sylvan deities, and to form sheltering places for those fairy beings during the frosts. The day after the sacrifices was kept as a day of rejoicing, neighbours visited each other with gifts, and with expressions of good will.

From all I have been able to gather respecting this great sun feast at the winter solstice as it was celebrated in this country in prehistoric times, I am of opinion that the sacrifices were offered to the sun on the shortest day, to propitiate his return, and that that day was a day of great solemnity, but that the day following when the mistletoe was distributed and hung up, was a day of rejoicing and thanksgiving on this account, that the sacrifices had proved acceptable and efficacious, the sun having returned again to begin his course for another year, and this day was the first day of the year.

I am aware that the Romans appointed the first of January as the first day of the year as early as B.C. 600, and dedicated it to the goddess *Stranæ*. This, however, could not affect the inhabitants of Britain, at least not until the Roman invasion, and this influence did not reach our northern counties. There can be little doubt, I think, that the great festival of the Romans, the Saturnalia, held in honour of *Saturn*, the father of the gods, and which lasting seven days, including the winter solstice, was introduced into this country, and in course of time became identified with the Druidical festival of the natives. Other elements conspired to modify the ancient druidical festival. After the Romans withdrew their armies from the island at the commencement of the fifth century, other invaders took their place. Saxons, Jutes, Angles, and Normans occupied large tracts of the country; but as these were mostly all sun-worshippers, their festivals and ceremonies would, for the most part, coincide with the native usages, and whatever peculiarities they might bring with them in the matter of formulas, would take root in the localities where they were settled, and eventually the indigenous and introduced formulas would coalesce. Another element which materially influenced and, *vice versa*, was materially influenced by Pagan formulæ, was Christianity. Introduced into Rome at a very early period, it was for a long time opposed as subversive of the established religion of the empire. Now, during

the festival of the Saturnalia, the Romans decorated their
houses, both inside and out, with evergreens, the Christian
converts refraining from this were easily discovered
and set upon by the people, were brought before the
judges and condemned, in many cases, to death, for their
infidelity to the national gods.   But as a result of this
severity the Christians learned to be politic, and during
the Saturnalia, hung evergreens round their houses, while
they kept festival within doors in commemoration of the
birth of Christ.   This Christian festival, with its heathen
attachments, soon spread throughout the Roman empire,
and thus became introduced into Britain also.   It appears
however, that the day on which this feast was kept differed
in different localities, until towards the middle of the fourth
century Julius I., Bishop of Rome, appointed the 25th
December as the festival day for the whole Church, an
edict which was universally obeyed.   As was to be expected, many of the ceremonies and superstitious beliefs
emanating from the Saturnalia were merged in the customs of the Christian feast, and do still survive in modified forms till the present day.   In many of our Christmas
customs we can thus perceive the influence of the self-
preservation policy of the early Roman Christians, and
in the survival of many other pagan customs in this
and other of our festivals, we can trace the influence
of another policy, the worldly-wise policy of the Roman
Church.

At the close of the sixth century, Pope Gregory sent St.
Augustine, or Austin, to this country as a missionary, and
by his preaching, many thousands of the people were
converted to Christianity.   This Pope's instructions to
Augustine concerning his treatment of heathen festivals,

were that "the heathen temples were not to be destroyed, but turned into Christian churches; that the oxen killed in sacrifice should still be killed with rejoicing, but their bodies given to the poor, and that the refreshment booths round the heathen temples should be allowed to remain as places of jollity and amusement for the people on Christian festivals, for it is impossible to cut abruptly from hard and rough minds all their old habits and customs. He who wishes to reach the highest place must rise by steps, and not by jumps."

From the enunciation of this policy, we can readily understand how the festive observances connected with heathen worship remained in the Christian observance. I have stated what is supposed to have been the Druidical manner of keeping this festival of the winter solstice, but I have not seen any account of how the festival was observed in this country when Augustine arrived as missionary. I have no information concerning the manner in which the oxen were sacrificed, nor the character of the refreshment booths round the temples. We know that there were booths in connection with heathen temples where women were kept, but whether this practice was indigenous in Britain, or was imported into this country by the Romans, or whether Pope Gregory may have written without any special knowledge of the customs here, but merely from his knowledge of heathen customs in general, we do not know. Nothing is said in these instructions about changing the day of keeping the festival from the solstice to the 25th of December. It is probable that no change of date was made at this time, at all events we may, from the following circumstance, infer that the change, if made, did not reach the northern

U

portion of the island. Haco, King of Norway, in the the tenth century fixed the 25th December as the day for keeping the feast of Yule. King Haco's fixing on this particular date would be a resultant from the Romish edict, for the Norwegians were at this time Christians, although their Christianity was a conglomerate of heathen superstition and church dogma.

According to Jamieson, the eve of Yule was termed by the Northmen *Hoggunott*, meaning Slaughter night, probably because then the cattle for the coming feast were killed. During the feast, one of the leading toasts was called *minnie*, meaning the cup of remembrance, and Dr. Jamieson thinks that the popular cry which has come down to our times as *Hogmany, trol-lol-lay*, was originally *Hogminne, thor loe loe*, meaning the feast of Thor. After the Reformation, the Scotch transferred Hogmanay to the last day of December, as a preparation day for the New Year. The practice of children going from door to door in little bands, singing the following rhyme, was in vogue at the beginning of this century in country places in the West of Scotland :—

> " Rise up, gudewife, and shake your feathers,
> Dinna think that we are beggars,
> We're girls and boys come out to-day,
> For to get our Hogmanay,
>   Hogmanay, trol-lol-lay.
>
> Give us of your white bread, and not of your gray,
> Or else we'll knock at your door a' day."

This rhyme has a stronger reference to Yule or Christmas than to the New Year, and is doubtless a relic of pre-Reformation times.

At the Reformation, the Scottish Church, probably

following the dictum of Calvin, who condemned Yule as a pagan festival, forbade the people to observe it because of its heathen origin; but probably the more potent reason was that it was a Romish feast, for no objection was made against keeping the New Year or *hansell Monday*, on which occasion practices similar to those of Yule were observed, and I believe it was the non-condemnation of these later festivals which enabled the Scottish Church to abolish Yule. In fact, it would appear that the Yule practices were simply transferred from a few days earlier to a few days later, and thereby retained their original connection with the close of the year. Prior to the Church interference there is no evidence that the first of January was observed by the people as a general feast, but even with this safety valve of a popular and yearly festival, the Church encountered great difficulty in abolishing Yule. A few instances of the opposition of the people will suffice.

The Glasgow Kirk Session, on the 26th December, 1583, had five persons before them who were ordered to make public repentance, because they kept the superstitious day called Yule. The *baxters* were required to give the names of those for whom they had baked Yule bread, so that they might be dealt with by the Church. Ten years after this, in 1593, an Act was again passed by the Glasgow Session against the keeping of Yule, and therein it was ordained that the keepers of this feast were to be debarred from the privileges of the Church, and also punished by the magistrates.

Notwithstanding these measures, the people still inclined to observe Yule, for fifty-six years after, in 1649, the General Assembly appointed a commission to make report of the public practices, among others, "The druidical customs observed at the fires of *Beltane, Midsummer, Hallowe'en*, and *Yule*." In the same year appears the following minute in the session-book of the Parish of Slains.—(See Rust's *Druidism Exhumed.*)

26th Nov., 1649.—"The said day, the minister and elders being convened in session, and after invocation of the name of God, intimate that Yule be not kept, but that they yoke their oxen and horse, and employ their servants in their service that day as well as on other work days."

Dr. Jamieson quotes the opinion of an English clergyman in reference to such proceedings of the Scotch Church :—"The ministers of Scotland, in contempt of the holy-day observed by England, cause their wives and servants to spin in open sight of the people upon Yule day, and their affectionate auditors constrain their servants to yoke their plough on Yule day, in contempt of Christ's nativity. Which our Lord has not left unpunished, for their oxen ran wud, and brak their necks and lamed some ploughmen, which is notoriously known in some parts of Scotland." By going back to the time of the Reformation, and finding what then were the practices of the people in the celebration of the Yule festival, and then by comparing these with the practices in vogue at the commencement of this century during the New Year festivities, we shall be led to conclude that the principal change effected by the Church was only respecting the time of the feasts, and we can thus perceive that the veto was not directed against the practices *per se*, but only against the conjunction of these practices, Pagan in their origin, with a feast commemorative of the birth of

Christ. As they could not hold Christmas without re-
taining the Yule practices along with it, they resolved to
abolish both.

Let us then pursue this retrospect and comparison.
About the time of the Reformation the day preceding
Yule was a day of general preparation. Houses were
cleaned out and borrowed articles were returned to their
owners. Work of all kind was stopped, and a general
appearance of completion of work was established; yarn
was reeled off, no lint was allowed to remain on the rock
of the wheel, and all work implements were laid aside.
In the evening cakes were baked, one for each person, and duly marked, and great care was taken
that none should break in the firing, as such an
accident was a bad omen for the person whose cake
met with the mishap. These cakes were eaten at
the Yule breakfast. A large piece of wood was placed
upon the fire in such time that it would be kindled
before twelve p.m., and extreme care was taken that
the fire should not go out, for not only was it unlucky,
but no one would oblige a neighbour, with a kindling
on Yule.

On Yule eve those possessing cattle went to the byre and
stable and repeated an *Ave Marie*, and a *Paternoster*, to
protect their cattle from an evil eye.

On Yule morning, attention was paid to the first person
who entered the house, as it was important to know
whether such a person were lucky or otherwise. It was
an unfriendly act to enter a house on Yule day without
bringing a present of some kind. Nothing was permitted to be taken out of the house on that day; this prohibition of course, did not extend to such things as were

taken for presents. Servants or members of the family who had gone out in the morning, when they returned to the house brought in with them something, although it might only be some trivial article, say for instance, garden stuff. This was done that they might bring, or, at least, not cause bad luck to the household. Masters or parents gave gifts to their servants and children, and owners of cattle gave their beasts, with their own hand their first food on Yule morning. After mass in church, a table was spread in the house with meat and drink, and all who entered were invited to partake. On this day neighbours and relations visited each other, bearing with them meat and drink warmed with condiments, and as they drank they expressed mutual wishes for each other's welfare. If not a Christian day, it was at least a day of good will to men. In the evening, the great family feast was held. In the more northern parts, where the Scandinavian national element was principally settled, a boar's head was the correct dish at this feast, and, by the better class, was always provided ; but the common people were content with venison, beef, and poultry, beginning their feast with a dish of plum porridge. A large candle, prepared for the occasion, was lighted at the commencement, and it was intended to keep in light till twelve p.m., and if it went out before it was regarded as a bad omen for the next year ; and what of it was left unconsumed at twelve o'clock was carefully laid past, to be used at the dead wake of the heads of the family.

Now, let us compare with this the practices current at Hogmanay (31st December), and New Year's Day, about the commencement of this century. In doing so, I will pass over without notice many superstitious observances which, though curious and interesting, belong rather to the general fund of superstitious belief than to the special festival at New Year, and confine myself to those which were peculiar to the time. In my grandfather's house, between sixty and seventy years ago, on the 31st December *(Hogmanay)*, all household work was stopped, rock emptied, yarn reeled and *hanked*, and wheel and reel put into an outhouse. The house itself was white-washed and cleaned. A block of wood or large piece of coal was put on the fire about ten p.m., so that it would be burning briskly before the household retired to bed. The last thing done by those who possessed a cow or horse was to visit the byre or stable, and I have been told that it was the practice with some, twenty years before my recollection, to say the Lord's Prayer during this visit. After rising on New Year's Day, the first care of those who possessed cattle was to visit the byre or stable, and with their own hands give the animals a feed. Burns followed this habit, and refers to it in one of his poems :—

> " A gude New Year I wish thee, Maggy,
> Hae, there's a rip to thy auld baggie."

The following was the practice in my father's house in Partick, between fifty and sixty years ago, on New Year's day :—On *Hogmanay* evening, children were all washed before going to bed. An oat bannock was baked for each child : it was nipped round the edge, had a hole in the centre, and was flavoured with carvey (carroway) seed. Great care was taken that none of these bannocks should break in the firing, as such an occurrence was regarded as a very unlucky omen for the child whose bannock was thus damaged. It denoted illness or death during the year. Parents sat up till about half-past eleven, when the fire was covered, and every particle of ash swept up and carried out of the house. All retired to bed before twelve o'clock, as it was unlucky not to be in bed as the New Year came in. A watchful eye was kept on the fire lest it should go out, for such an event was regarded as very unlucky, and they would neither give nor receive a light from any one on New Year's day. Neither fire, ashes, nor anything belonging to the house was taken out of it on that day. In the morning we children got our bannocks to breakfast. They were small, and it was unlucky to leave any portion of them, although this was frequently done. The first-foot was an important episode. To visit empty-handed on this day was tantamount to wishing a curse on the family. A plane-soled person was an unlucky first-foot; a pious sanctimonious person was not good, and a hearty ranting merry fellow was considered the best sort of first-foot. It was necessary for luck that what was poured out of the first-foot's gift, be it whiskey or other drink, should be drunk to the dregs by each recipient, and it was requisite that he should do the same by their's. It was against rule for any portion to be left, but if there did happen to be an unconsumed remnant, it was cast out. With any subsequent visitor these particulars were not observed. I remember that one year our first-foot was a man who had fallen and broken his bottle, and cut and bleeding was assisted into our house. My mother made up her mind that this was a most unfortunate first-foot, and that something serious would occur in the family during that year. I believe had the whole family been cut off, she would not have been surprised. However, it was a prosperous year, and a bleeding first-foot was not afterwards considered bad. If anything extraordinary did occur throughout the year, it was remembered and referred to afterwards. One New Year's day something was stolen out of our house; that year father and mother were confined to bed for weeks; the cause and effect were quite clear. During the day neighbours visited each other with bottle and bun, every one overflowing with good wishes. In the evening the family, old and young, were gathered together, those who during the year were out at service, the married with their families, and at this meal the best the family could afford was produced. It was a happy time, long looked forward to, and long remembered by all.

BELTANE.

Beltane or Beilteine means *Baal's fire*, Baal (Lord) was the name under which the Phœnicians recognized their primary male god, the Sun : fire was his earthly symbol and the medium through which sacrifices to him were offered. Hence sun and fire-worship were identical. I am of opinion that originally the Beltane festival was held at the Spring equinox but that its original connection with the equinox, in process of time was forgotten, and it became a festival inaugurative of summer. There is some difference of opinion as to the particular day on

which the Beltane festival was held in this country.   Dr.
Jamieson, Dr. R. Chambers, and others who have studied
this subject say that the 1st May (old style) was Beltane
day.   Professor Veitch; in his *History und Poetry of the
Scottish Border*, (p. 118,) says, speaking of the Druids :—
They worshipped the sun god, the representative of
the bright side of nature—Baal, the fire-giver—and
to him on the hill tops they lit the fire on the end of
May, the Beltane."   And again, in his remarks on
Peblis to the Play, (p. 315,) he says :—"The play was not the
name for a stage play, but indicated the sports and
festivals which took place at Peebles annually at Beltane, the second of May, not the first of May, as is
usually supposed.   These had in all probability come
in place of the ancient British practice of lighting fires
on the hill tops in honour of Baal, the sun god, hence
the name *Baaltein*, Beltane, *i.e.* Baal's fire.   The
Christian Church had so far modified the ceremonial
as to substitute for the original idolatrous practice
that of a day of rustic amusements.   A fair or market
at the same period which lasted for eight days had also
been instituted by Royal charter.   But even the practice of lighting fires on the hill tops was late in dying
out, with the usual tenacity of custom it survived for
long all memory of its original meaning."

The Professor writes very positively as to Beltane day
being the second day of May, not the first day as is supposed.   The Royal Charter granted to the Burgh of
Peebles for holding a fair or market on Beltane day, is
given in the Burgh Records of Peebles, p. 85 :—" As also
·of holding, using, enjoying, and exercising within the
foresaid Burgh weekly market days according to the use

and custom of the said Burgh, together with three fairs, thrice in the year, the first thereof beginning yearly upon the third day of May, called Beltane day, the same to be held and continued for the space of forty-eight hours thereafter." The date of the Charter is 1621, but it is evident that the third of May had been previously kept as Beltane day. The Professor is also mistaken in stating that the Beltane fair of Peebles was to be kept for eight days. The third fair, held in August, continued eight days, but the fairs in May and June were kept for two days according to the Charter. That there were two days known as Beltane at the beginning of last century is evident from a book of Scotch proverbs published in 1721 by James Kelly, A.M., in which occurs the following,—

> " You have skill of man and beast,
> Ye was born between the Beltans."

In all probability the discrepancy as to the day originated through the Church substituting a Christian festival for a heathen one; and although the date was changed, yet through force of custom the name of the old festival was retained, and in localities where the power of the Church was comparatively weak, the older, the original day for the festival would probably be kept as well as the newly appointed Church festival. This view of the matter is rendered probable from the fact that the Church did institute a great festival, to be held on the third of May, to commemorate the finding of the cross of Christ. The legend is as follows :—When the Empress Helena was at Jerusalem about the end of the third century, she discovered the cross on which Christ was crucified, and had it conveyed to the great church built by Constantine her son. This cross was exhibited yearly to the people, and many miracles were wrought by it. A festival, as I have said, was instituted in commemoration of the discovery, and this was held on the third of May, and was called *Rood* or *rude* day. Churches were built and dedicated to the Holy Rood, among which was that which is now Holyrood Palace. Where the Church was powerful, as in Edinburgh and Peebles, Rood day would be the important festival, and Beltane would gradually become incorporated with it, the names Beltane day and Rood day becoming synonymous. Thus we may account for Edinburgh and Peebles keeping Beltane on the third day of May, while in Perth and other northern counties where the Church influence was .weaker, the festival would be kept according to the older custom on the first of May.

In Druidical times the people allowed their fires to go out on Beltane eve, and on Beltane day the priests met on a hill dedicated to the Sun, and obtained fire from heaven. When the fire was obtained, sacrifices were offered, and the people danced round the fire with shoutings till the sacrifices were consumed; after which they received portions of the sacred fire with which to re-kindle their hearths for another twelve months. Besides mountains, there were evidently other localities where sacrifices and the ritual of Sun-worship were observed, and which received appropriate names in accordance with their character as sacred places. Some of these names still survive, as for instance :—

Ard-an-teine—The light of the fire.

Craig-an-teine—The rock of the fire.

Auch-an-teine—The field of the fire.

Tillie-bet-teine—The knoll of the fire ; and so through a great many other names of places we find traces of the Baal and fire worship. So widespread and numerous are the names which recall this ritual, that we can see quite clearly that the spirit of their religion thoroughly dominated the people. In Ireland, at Beltane, the Pagan Kings are said to have convoked the people for State purposes. The last of these heathen kings convoked a grand assembly of the nation to meet with him on *Tara*, at the feast of Beltane, which the old chroniclers say was the principal feast of the year.

Respecting this feast, Dr. Jamieson says, introducing a quotation from O'Brien, "*Ignis Bei Dei Aseatica ea line-heil*, or May-day, so called from large fires which the Druids were used to light on the summits of the highest hills, into which they drove four-footed beasts, using certain ceremonies to expiate for the sins of the people. The Pagan ceremony of lighting these fires in honour of the Asiatic god Belus gave its name to the entire month of May, which to this day is called *Me-na-bealtine*, in the Irish, *Dor Keating*." He says again, speaking of these fires of *Baal*, that the cattle were driven through them and not sacrificed, the chief design being to avert contagious disorders from them for the year. And quoting from an ancient glossary, O'Brien says, "The Druids lighted two solemn fires every year, and drove all four-footed beasts through them, in order to preserve them from contagious distempers during the current year." I am inclined to think that these notices describe a sort of modified or Christianized Beltane, that driving the cattle through the fire was a substitute for the older form of sacrificing cattle to the sun. Until very lately in different parts of Ireland, it was the common practice to kindle fires in milking yards on the first day of May, and then men, women, and children leaped through them, and the cattle were driven through in order to avert evil influences. They were also in the habit of quenching their fires on the last day of April, and rekindling them on the first day of May. In certain localities in Perthshire, so lately as 1810, (I have referred to this before), the inhabitants collected and kindled a fire by friction, and through the fire thus kindled they drove their cattle in order to protect them against disease, and at the same time they held a feast of rejoicing.

As already mentioned, the Romans held several festivals at the beginning of summer, and many of their observances on these occasions were introduced into this country, and became incorporated with the Beltane practices. For example, the Romans held a festival in honour of *Pales*, the goddess of flocks and sheepfolds. The feast was termed *Palilia*. Lempriere states that some of the ceremonies accompanying the feast consisted in " burning heaps of straw, and in leaping over them ; no sacrifices were offered, but purifications were made with the smoke of horse's blood, and with the ashes of a calf that had been taken from the belly of its mother after it had been sacrificed, and with the ashes of beans ; the purification of the flocks was also made with the smoke of sulphur, also of the olive, the pine, the laurel, and rosemary. Offerings of mild cheese, boiled wine, and cakes of millet were afterwards made. Some call this festival *Palilia*, because the sacrifices were offered to the divinity for the fecundity of their flocks." There was also a large cake prepared for *Pales*, and a prayer was addressed to the divinity by shepherds, as thus given by Dr. Jamieson :—

> " O let me propitious find,
> And to the shepherd and his sheep be kind ;
> Far from my flocks drive noxious things away,
> And let my flocks in wholesome pastures stray.
> May I, at night, my morning's number take,
> Nor mourn a theft the prowling wolf may make.
> May all my rams the ewes with vigour press,
> To give my flocks a yearly due increase."

The Romans held another festival in honour of the goddess *Flora*. It began on the 28th April, and lasted three days. The people wore garlands of flowers, and carried them about with branches of newly-budded trees. There was much licentiousness connected with this feast.

Reference has already been made to another Roman festival which was celebrated early in May. This was called the *Lamuralia*, and its purport was to propitiate the favour of the ghosts or spirits of their ancestors. I am of opinion that the English May feasts are a survival of the *Floralia*, and, as kept 'during the middle ages, were not free from some of the indecencies of the *Floralia*. In my remembrance, the first of May, in the country west of Glasgow, was honoured by decking the houses with tree branches and flowers. Horses were also similarly decked. The Church did not attempt to abolish these heathen festivals, but endeavoured to dominate them, and substitute for legends of heathen

origin connected with them legends of Church origin.
In this they partly succeeded. The following account of
the Beltane festival, as it was kept in some districts in
Perthshire at the close of last century, taken from the
statistical accounts of certain parishes, will shew how
persistent these ancient customs were, and also how some
other festivals latterly became amalgamated and identified with Beltane :—

"In the Parish of Callander, upon the first day of
May," says the minister of the parish, "all the boys in
the town or hamlet meet on the moors. They cut a
table on the green sod, of a round shape, to hold the
whole company. They kindle a fire, and dress a re-
past of eggs and milk in the consistence of a custard.
They knead a cake of oatmeal, which is baked at the
fire upon a stone. After the custard is eaten up, they
divide the cake into as many portions, and as similar
as possible, as there are persons in the company.
They blacken one of these portions with char-
coal until it is perfectly black. They put all the
bits of cake into a bonnet. Every one blindfolded draws
a portion—he who holds the bonnet is entitled to the
last. Who draws the black bit is the devoted person to
be sacrificed to Baal, whose favour they mean to implore
in rendering the year productive of substance for man
and beast. There is little doubt of these human sacrifices being once offered in the country, but the youth
who has got the black bit must leap through the flame of
the fire three times." I have myself conversed with old
men who, when boys, were present at, and took part in
these observances ; and they told me that in their grandfathers' time it was the men who practised these rites,

but as they were generally accompanied with much drinking and riot, the clergy set their faces against the customs, and subjected the parties observing them to church discipline, so that in course of time the practices became merely the frolic of boys.

In the Parish of Logierait, Beltane is celebrated by the shepherds and cowherds in the following manner. They assemble in the fields and dress a dinner of milk and eggs. This dish they eat with a sort of cake baked for the occasion, having small lumps or nipples raised all over its surface. These knobs are not eaten, but broken off, and given as offerings to the different supposed powers or influences that protect or destroy their flocks, to the one as a thank-offering, to the other as a peace-offering.

Mr. Pennant, in his *Tour through Scotland*, thus describes the Beltane observances as they were observed at the end of last century. "The herds of every village hold their Beltane (a rural sacrifice.) They cut a square trench in the ground, leaving the turf in the middle. On that they make a fire of wood, on which they dress a large caudle of eggs, oatmeal, butter, and milk, and bring besides these plenty of beer and whiskey. Each of the company must contribute something towards the feast. The rites begin by pouring a little of the caudle upon the ground, by way of a libation. Every one then takes a cake of oatmeal, on which are raised nine square knobs, each dedicated to some particular being who is supposed to preserve their herds, or to some animal the destroyer of them. Each person then turns his face to the fire, breaks off a knob, and, flinging it over his shoulder, says—' *This I give to thee,*' naming the being whom he thanks, ' *preserver of my sheep,*' &c. ; or

w

to the destroyer, '*This I give to thee, (O fox or eagle),*' *spare my lambs,*' &c. When this ceremony is over they all dine on the caudle."

The shepherds in Perthshire still hold a festival on the 1st of May, but the practices at it are now much modified.

As may readily be surmised, there were a great many superstitious beliefs connected with Beltane, some of which still survive, and tend to maintain its existence. Dew collected on the morning of the first day of May is supposed to confer witch power on the gatherer, and give protection against an evil eye. To be seen in a field at day-break that morning, rendered the person seen an object of fear. A story is told of a farmer who, on the first of May discovered two old women in one of his fields, drawing a hair rope along the grass. On being seen, they fled. The farmer secured the rope, took it home with him, and hung it in the byre. When the cows were milked every spare dish about the farm-house was filled with milk, and yet the udders remained full. The farmer being alarmed, consigned the rope to the fire, and then the milk ceased to flow.

It was believed that first of May dew preserved the skin from wrinkles and freckles, and gave a glow of youth. To this belief Ferguson refers in the following lines :—

> " On May day in a fairy ring,
> We've seen them round St. Anthon's spring,
> Frae grass the caller dew to wring,
>   To wet their een ;
> And water clear as crystal spring,
>   To synd them clean."

MIDSUMMER.

To sun worshippers no season would be better calculated to excite devotional feelings towards the great luminary than the period when he attained the zenith of his strength. It is probable, therefore, that as his movements must have been closely observed, and his various phases regarded by the people, in the language of Scripture, "for signs and for seasons, for days and for years," that the turning points in the sun's yearly course, the solstices, would naturally become periods of worship. That the Summer solstice was an important religious period is rendered probable from the following curious observation concerning Stonehenge, which appeared in the Notes and Queries portion of the *Scotsman* newspaper for July 31, 1875. The *Scotsman's* correspondent states that "a party of Americans went on midsummer morning this year to see the sun rise upon Stonehenge. They found crowds of people assembled. Stonehenge," continues the writer, "may roughly be described as comprising seven-eighths of a circle, from the open ends of which there runs eastward an avenue having upright stones on either side. At some distance beyond this avenue, but in a direct line with its centre, stands one solitary stone in a sloping position ; in front of which, but at a considerable distance, is an eminence or hill. The point of observation chosen by the excursion party was the stone table or altar near the head of, and within the circle, directly looking down. The morning was unfavourable, but, fortunately, just as the sun was beginning to appear over the top of the hill, the mist disappeared, and then, for a few moments, the onlookers stood amazed at the spectacle presented to their view. While it lasted, the sun, like an immense ball, appeared actually to rest on the isolated stone of which mention has been made. Now, in this," says a writer in the *New Quarterly Magazine* for January, 1876, commenting upon the statement of the *Scotsman's* correspondent, "we find strong proof that Stonehenge was really a mighty almanack in stone; doubtless also a temple of the sun, erected by a race which has long perished without intelligible record."

I think it is not a very fanciful supposition to suppose, from the still existing names of places in this country bearing reference to sun-worship, that there were other places than Stonehenge which were used as stone almanacks "for signs and for seasons," and also for temples. *Grenach* in Perthshire, meaning *Field of the Sun*, where there is a large stone circle, may have been such a place; and *Grian-chnox*, now Greenock, meaning *Knoll of the Sun*, may have originally marked the place where the sun's rising became visible at a certain period of the year, from a stone circle in the neighbourhood. As far as I have been able to discover, there remains to us little trace of the manner in which the midsummer feast was kept in this country in prehistoric times, but so far as traces do remain, they appear to indicate that it was celebrated much after the same manner as the Scottish Celts are said to have celebrated Beltane. Indeed, the Celtic Irish hold their *Beilteme* feast on the 21st June, and their fires are kindled on the tops of hills, and each member of a family is, in order to secure good luck, obliged to pass through the fire. On this occasion also, a feast is held. A similar practice was common in West Cornwall at midsummer. Fires were kindled, and the people danced round them, and leaped singly through the flames to ensure good luck and protection against witchcraft. The following passage occurs in *Traditions and Hearthside Stories of West Cornwall*, by William Bottreill, 1873 :—" Many years ago, on Midsummer eve, when it became dusk, very old people in the west country would hobble away to some high ground whence they obtained a view of the most prominent high hill, such as Bartinney-Chapel, Cambrae, Sancras Bickan, Castle-au-dinas, Cam-Gulver, St. Agnes-Bickan, and many other beacon hills far away to the north and east which vied with each other in their midsummer night blaze. They counted the fires, and drew a presage from the number of them. There are now but few bonfires to be seen on the western heights ; yet we have observed that Tregonan, Godolphin, and Carn-warth hills, with others far away towards Redruth, still retain their Baal fires. We would gladly go many miles to see the weird-looking, yet picturesque dancers around the flames, on a cairn or high hill top, as we have seen them some forty years ago." The ancient Egyptians had their midsummer feasts, as also had the Greeks and Romans. During these festivals, we are told that the people, headed by the priests, walked in procession, carrying flowers and other emblems of the season in honour of their gods. Such processions were continued during the early years of the Christian Church, and the Christian priests in their vestments went into the fields to ask a blessing on the agricultural produce of the year. Towards the beginning of the twelfth century the Church introduced the *Feast of God*, and fixed the 19th June for its celebration. The eucharistic elements were declared to be the actual presence of God, and this, the consecrated Host or God himself was carried through the open streets by a procession of priests, the people turning out to do it honour, kneeling and worshipping as it passed. This feast of God may have absorbed some of the ancient midsummer practices, but the *Feast of St. John's Day*, which is held upon the 24th June, has in its customs a greater similarity to the ancient sun feast. On the eve of St. John's day, people went to the woods and brought home branches of trees, which they fixed over their doorways. Towards night of St. John's Day, bonfires were kindled, and round them the people danced with frantic mirth, and men and boys leaped through the flames. Leaping through the flames is a common practice at these survivals of sun festivals, and although done now, partly for luck and partly for sport, there can be little doubt but that originally human sacrifices were then offered to the sun god.

There was quite a host of curious superstitions connected with this midsummer feast, especially in Ireland and Germany, and many of these were similar to those connected with the feast of *Halloween* in Scotland. In Ireland, in olden times, it was believed that the souls of people left their sleeping bodies, and visited the place where death would ultimately overtake them ; and there were many who, in consequence, would not sleep, but sat up all night. People also went out on St. John's eve to gather certain plants which were held as sacred, such as *the rose, the trifoil, St. John's wort,* and *vervain,* the possession of which gave them influence over evil. To catch the seed of the fern as it fell to the ground on St. John's eve, exactly at twelve o'clock, was believed to confer upon the persons who caught it the power of rendering themselves invisible at will.

In my opinion, the great prehistoric midsummer festival to the sun god has diverged into the two Church feasts, Eucharist and St. John's day ; but St. John's day has absorbed the greater share of old customs and superstitious ideas, and so numerous are they that the most meagre description of them would yield matter for an hour's reading.

HALLOWE'EN.

The northern nations, like the Hebrews, began their day in the evening. Thus we have Yule Eve, and Hallow Eve (Hallowe'en), the evenings preceding the respective feasts. The name Hallowe'en is of Christian origin, but the origin of the feast itself is hidden in ancient mythology. The Celtic name for the autumn festival was *Sham-in*, meaning Baal's Fire. The Irish Celts called it *Sainhain*, or *Sainfuin; Sain*, summer, and *Fuin*, end,—*i.e.*, the end of summer. The Hebrews and Phœnicians called this festival *Baal-Shewin*, a name signifying the principle of order. The feast day in Britain and Ireland is the first of November. The Druids are said on this day to have sacrificed horses to the sun, as a thank-offering for the harvest. An Irish king, who reigned 400 A.D., commanded sacrifices to be made to a moon idol, which was worshipped by the people on the evening of *Sain-hain*. Sacrifices were also offered on this night to the spirits of the dead, who were believed to have liberty at this season to visit their old earthly haunts and their friends,—a belief this, which was entertained by many ancient nations, and was the origin of many of the curious superstitious customs still extant in this country on Hallowe'en. Dr. Smith, commenting in *Jamieson's Dictionary* on the solemnities of

Beltane, says, "The other of these solemnities was held upon Hallow Eve, which in Gælic still retains the name of *Sham-in*,—this word signifying the Fire of Peace, or the time of kindling the fire for maintaining peace. It was at this season that the Druids usually met in the most central places of every country to adjust every dispute and decide every controversy. On that occasion, all the fires in the country were extinguished on the preceding evening, in order to be supplied next day by a portion of the holy fire which was kindled and consecrated by the Druids. Of this, no person who had infringed the peace, or become obnoxious by any breach of law, or guilty of any failure in duty, was to have share, till he had first made all the reparation and submission which the Druids required of him. Whoever did not, with the most implicit obedience, agree to this, had the sentence of excommunication passed against him, which was more dreaded than death; none being allowed to give him house or fire, or shew him the least office of humanity, under the penalty of incurring the same sentence." The ancient Romans held a great and popular festival at the end of February, called the *Ferralia*. At this season, they visited the graves of their departed friends, and offered sacrifices and oblations to the spirits of the dead; they believed that the spirits of the departed, both the good and the bad, were released on that particular night, and that, if they were not propitiated, these spirits would haunt throughout the coming year their undutiful living relatives. In all probability, though the time of celebration is different, these Roman ceremonies and the Hallowe'en ceremonies in this country had a common origin. In the year 610, the Bishop of Rome ordained that the heathen Pantheon should be converted into a Christian church, and dedicated to all the martyrs ; and a festival was instituted to commemorate the event. This was held on the first of May, and continued to be held on this day till 834, when the time of celebration was altered to the first of November, and it was then called *All Hallow*, from a Saxon word, *Haligan*, meaning to keep holy. This change was doubtless made in order to supply a Christian substitute for some heathen festival—in all probability the festival of *Sham-in*, which, as we have seen, was an old Druidical feast. Some time after this alteration in the time of holding the feast in honour of the martyrs, in 993, another festival was instituted for the purpose of offering prayers for the souls of those in purgatory, and this feast was kept on the second of November, and was called *All Souls*. The following legend was either invented as a plausible reason for instituting this additional feast, or the legend, being previously well known and accepted as truth, was really the *bona fide* reason for the institution : —" A pilgrim, returning from the Holy Land, was compelled by storm to land upon a rocky island, where he found a hermit, who told him that among the cliffs of the island was an opening into the infernal regions, through which huge flames ascended, and where the groans of the tormented were distinctly audible. The pilgrim, on his return, told the Abbot of Clugny of this, and the Abbot appointed the second day of November to be set apart for the benefit of souls in purgatory, which was to be kept by prayers and almsgiving." It is easy to perceive that, while in the

x

festival of Hallowe'en we have the survival of the old
Druidical festival of thank-offering to the sun-god for the
ingathering of the fruits of the earth, we have also in
these two festivals of *All Saints* and *All Souls* the survival of the ancient *Ferralia*, or festival to the dead,
when offerings were made to both good and bad spirits,
to prevent them haunting the living ; and thus we can
account for the prevalence of the numerous superstitions
concerning ghosts and evil spirits connected with the
festival of Hallowe'en.   That these Church feasts were
regarded as the substitute for the *Ferralia* of Pagan
Rome is verified by Father Meagan in his work on *The
Mass.* We quote from Jamieson :—" Such was the devotion of the heathen on this day by offering sacrifices
for the souls in purgatory, by praying at the graves,
and performing processions round the churchyards
with lighted tapers, that they called the month the
month of pardons, indulgences, and absolutions for
souls in purgatory; or, as Plutarch calls it, the purifying month, or season of purification, because the living
and dead were supposed to be purged and purified on
these occasions from their sins by sacrifices, flagellations,
and other works of mortification."   Plutarch, I think,
must have referred to the month of February as the
purifying month.   Father Meagan has not referred to
the change of date made by the Church.   Doubtless the
Christian Church, in instituting these festivals, intended,
by divesting them of their heathen basis, to christianise
the people ; but, like Naaman of old, the worshippers,
while they worshipped in the buildings in conformity
with the regulations of their new teachers, yet retained
many of their old Pagan beliefs and ceremonies, and

even their teachers were not thoroughly de-Paganised,—and so the old and new commingled and crystallized together.

In all the four festivals we have been considering, there survive relics of fire-worship, and through all there runs a similarity of observance and belief; but the special practices are not everywhere joined to the same festival in all localities. In this part of the country, the special observances connected with Hallowe'en were, in other parts of the country, observed in connection with the summer festival. Now, however, we are glad to say, these superstitious ceremonies and beliefs in their old gross forms are fast passing away, or have become so modified that we can scarcely recognise their relations to the old fire-worship.

In 1860, I was residing near the head of Loch Tay during the season of the Hallowe'en feast. For several days before Hallowe'en, boys and youths collected wood and conveyed it to the most prominent places on the hill sides in their neighbourhood. Some of the heaps were as large as a corn-stack or hay-rick. After dark on Hallowe'en, these heaps were kindled, and for several hours both sides of Loch Tay were illuminated as far as the eye could see. I was told by old men that at the beginning of this century men as well as boys took part in getting up the bonfires, and that, when the fire was ablaze, all joined hands and danced round the fire, and made a great noise; but that, as these gatherings generally ended in drunkenness and rough and dangerous fun, the ministers set their faces against the observance, and were seconded in their efforts by the more intelligent and well-behaved in the community; and so the practice was discontinued by adults and relegated to school boys. In the statistical account of the parish of Callender, the same practice is referred to. It is stated that " When the bonfire was consumed, the ashes of the fire were carefully collected in the form of a circle, and a stone put in near the circumference for every person in the several families concerned in getting up the fire; and whatever stone is moved out its place or injured before next morning, the person represented by the stone is devoted or fey, and is supposed not to live twelve months from that day." In all probability this devoted person was in olden times offered as a sacrifice to the fire god on the great day of sacrifice, which was the festival day. The belief that the spirits of the dead were free to roam about on that night is still held by many in this country. Indeed, where the forms of the feast have all but disappeared, the superstitious auguries connected with it survive. Burns particularises very fully the formulæ of Halloween, as practised in Ayrshire in his day, and as this poem is well known, it would be superfluous to follow it in detail here; but I cannot refrain from drawing attention to the suggestions which one of the practices which he mentions affords in favour of the supposition that it is a relic of an ancient form of appeal to the fire god—I refer to the practice of burning nuts. It seems likely that in ancient times the priests, who claimed prophetic power through the reading of auguries, used this method of deciding the future at this particular season of the year, and chiefly during the holding of the feast.

Although I have confined my remarks to the four

feasts, Yule, Beltane, Midsummer, and Halloween, because they are the oldest and most properly national, there were a number of other heathen feasts, emanating principally from Roman practice, which the Church converted into Christian feasts, notably what is now called Candlemass. On the second day of February, the Romans perambulated their city with torches and candles burning in honour of *Februa;* and the Greeks at this same period held their feast of lights in honour of Ceres. Pope Innocent explains the origin of this feast of Candlemass. He states that "The heathens dedicated this month to the infernal gods. At its beginning Pluto stole away Proserpine, and her mother Ceres sought for her in the night with lighted torches. In the beginning of this month the idolaters walked about the city with lighted candles, and as some of the holy fathers could not extirpate such a custom, they ordained that Christians should carry about candles in honour of the Virgin Mary." This method of keeping the feast of Candlemass does not now prevail in this country; so far as the laity are concerned, the festival may be said to have died out, but according to Dr. Brewer, the festival is kept by the Roman Catholic Church as the time for consecrating the candles used in the Church service.

Formerly there were other public festivals, as Lammas, Michaelmass, &c., which the Church had substituted for heathen feasts which have ceased to be public festivals, and I trust we may indulge the hope that the time is not far distant when, instead of all such festive relics of heathenism, the Church and people will substitute one daily festival of obedience to the honour of the founder of Christianity, viz., the festival of a righteous life.

INDEX.

Y

190   INDEX.